THE WEST AT WAR

U.S. and European Counterterrorism Efforts, Post–September 11

Michael Jacobson

THE WASHINGTON INSTITUTE FOR NEAR EAST POLICY

Published in 2006 in the United States of America by the Washington Institute for Near East Policy, 1828 L Street NW, Suite 1050, Washington, D.C. 20036.

Library of Congress Cataloging-in-Publication Data

Jacobson, Michael, 1969–
    The West at war : U.S. and European counterterrorism efforts, post–September 11 / Michael Jacobson.
    p. cm.
    ISBN 1-933162-00-7
    1. Terrorism—United States. Terrorism—Europe. 3. Terrorism—Prevention—United States. 4. Terrorism—Prevention—Europe. 5. War on Terrorism, 2001– 6. September 11 Terrorist Attacks, 2001. I. Title.
    HV6432.J36 2006
    363.325'17—dc22

                                                              2006008638

Design by Daniel Kohan, Sensical Design & Communication
Front cover: Copyright AP Wide World Photos/Matt Dunham

About the Author

Michael Jacobson is a senior advisor at the U.S. Department of the Treasury. This book was written during his tenure as a Soref fellow at The Washington Institute, from September 2004 to June 2005. Prior to joining the Institute, he served as counsel on both the 9-11 Commission and the House-Senate Joint Inquiry into the September 11 attacks, focusing on the plot itself, the performance of the FBI, and associated domestic intelligence policy issues. Previously, he worked at the FBI for five years, first joining the bureau as a presidential management intern in 1997. While there, he worked as an intelligence analyst in the National Security Division and as an assistant general counsel in the Office of the General Counsel.

Mr. Jacobson holds a bachelor's degree in psychology from Brandeis University, a juris doctor from the Boston College Law School, and a master's degree in international relations from the Fletcher School at Tufts University.

■ ■ ■

Table of Contents

Acknowledgments vii

Foreword ix

Author's Note xiii

Executive Summary xv

Introduction 1

1. The Importance of European Counterterrorism to U.S.
   National Security 5

2. From Reaction to Prevention 27

3. Mixed Results with the Preventive Approach 76

4. Obstacles to Successful Terrorism Prosecution 100

Conclusion 128

Acknowledgments

THIS MONOGRAPH WAS WRITTEN DURING A NINE-month period while I was working as a Soref fellow at The Washington Institute. The text is based on open source information—including books, law reviews, and other journals, magazines, and newspapers—and, most important, on interviews I conducted during my time at the Institute. I interviewed approximately seventy-five people during the course of my research, both in the United States and Europe. In the United States, I interviewed a wide variety of experts in the field, including many current and former U.S. government officials, think tank fellows, and academics. I also spent two weeks conducting interviews in Europe in early 2005, speaking with a broad range of people, including academics and researchers. I was particularly fortunate to have the opportunity to interview many current British, German, and European Union counterterrorism officials.

My thoughts on this topic were also shaped by my colleagues at The Washington Institute, particularly Matthew Levitt and Patrick Clawson, who provided able guidance throughout the process. I am indebted to my two research assistants, Deanna Befus and Lucinda Brown, without whom this project would have been difficult—if not impossible—to complete. Thanks are also due to Robert Satloff for giving me the opportunity to work at the Institute.

Foreword

AS A MEMBER OF THE NATIONAL COMMISSION ON Terrorist Attacks upon the United States (commonly known as the 9-11 Commission) and the Joint House-Senate September 11 Inquiry, I spent nearly two-and-a-half years investigating the events of September 2001. Like my colleagues, I believed that a fair, vigorous inquiry was essential to determining whether the attacks could have been prevented and what governmental changes were needed as a result.

Throughout that period, I worked closely with Michael Jacobson, one of the few staff members to serve as counsel on both investigations. He played a key role in the investigation of the FBI's counterterrorism efforts and the September 11 plot itself. Within the Joint Inquiry, he served on the investigative team that uncovered a series of significant pre–September 11 FBI failures. These included the infamous "Phoenix memo," in which an Arizona-based FBI agent wrote headquarters in July 2001 regarding a number of concerns, such as suspected al-Qaeda members engaging in flight training; FBI headquarters' misunderstanding of the Foreign Intelligence Surveillance Act (FISA) and unwillingness to push for a FISA warrant in the investigation of Zacarias Moussaoui, despite protests from the Minneapolis FBI office; and the eventual hijackers' contact with numerous individuals known to the bureau, including an FBI informant. In his book *Intelligence Matters*, Senator Bob Graham, co-chair of the Joint Inquiry, credited Jacobson for the latter discovery, referring to it as "remarkable investigative sleuthing."

While serving on the 9-11 Commission, Jacobson aggressively followed up on his work with the Joint Inquiry. He faced a particularly daunting task while working on a team tasked with piecing together the September 11 plot, which involved absorbing the massive amount of information the government had already gathered while conducting additional investigations to complete the story. Following evidentiary trails wherever they led, Jacobson and his fellow team members traveled to the Middle East, Europe, and throughout the United States, reviewing documents, interviewing the hijackers' associates, and familiarizing themselves with the neighborhoods in which the terrorists lived. In the end, the commissioners and staff succeeded beyond what many thought was possible, producing a riveting, definitive report on the September 11 plot and garnering a National Book Award nomination.

Jacobson brings many of these same investigative skills to bear in this new and timely monograph on U.S. and European counterterrorism efforts. The book expands on the work of the Joint Inquiry and 9-11 Commission in several respects. While those investigations analyzed the FBI's intelligence capabilities in the war on terror, Jacobson's study evaluates both FBI and Justice Department counterterrorism efforts from a law-enforcement perspective, focusing on America's ability to prosecute suspected terrorists. The book also explores how the role of law enforcement has evolved since September 11 and assesses the effectiveness of these changes.

The 9-11 Commission and Joint Inquiry also regarded European counterterrorism efforts as important areas of investigation. After all, it is well known that three of the principal hijackers lived in Hamburg, Germany, before moving to the United States to train and carry out the attacks. As part of the investigation of this "Hamburg cell," Jacobson traveled to Germany twice, representing first the Joint Inquiry and then the 9-11 Commission. During the course of these and other investigations, we determined that the German government faced significant legal barriers prior to September 11 that restricted its ability to investigate Islamist terrorist activity. We also concluded that the German government had not considered Islamist terrorist groups a serious threat and was unwilling to devote resources to targeting them. In this monograph, Jacobson describes the numerous steps that Germany has since taken—including legislative and structural changes—to tackle the systemic problems exposed by the September 11 attacks. Despite these changes, he notes, Germany continues to face serious difficulties in its efforts to prosecute suspected terrorists, similar to the United States and Britain.

The 9-11 Commission also examined law enforcement systems overseas as part of its effort to determine whether the FBI should retain primary jurisdiction over domestic counterterrorism. Britain received special attention because of the similarities between its legal system and our own, and because of the stellar reputation of its domestic intelligence agency, MI-5. In fact, for a time, many U.S. lawmakers, outside experts, and media outlets framed questions relating to U.S. domestic intelligence in terms of whether America needed its own version of MI-5. Jacobson's monograph goes further and examines the changing relationship between MI-5 and British law enforcement entities. He shows, for example, how the traditional barriers between intelligence and law enforcement in Britain are being broken down, as they are in Germany and the United States. This type of comparative analysis would have been very useful to the 9-11 Commission as it formulated its domestic intelligence policy recommendations.

The monograph also helps illustrate another vital lesson of September 11: that terrorists based in Europe can have a dramatic impact on U.S. national security. Terrorist activity has only increased in Europe during the time period covered by this study (from the September 11 attacks to June 2005). More recent events, including the London bombings and the disruption of numerous terrorist cells by European authorities over the past year, all confirm Jacobson's conclusion that "Europe has become one of the most important battlegrounds in the global fight against Islamist terrorism."

For centuries, the surest course for national security involved accumulating military power and using diplomatic skill to build alliances that would deter attack. Now, however, the actions of al-Qaeda and other jihadists have shown us with stunning clarity that new strategies are needed. Policymakers in both Europe and the United States should pay close attention to new ideas. The policy prescriptions offered in this monograph are straightforward, reasonable, and achievable; implementing them would be an important step toward strengthening our security and restoring a sense of safety for Americans wherever they reside or travel.

Tim Roemer
Former congressman and 9-11 Commission member

Author's Note

THIS BOOK IS INTENDED AS A TIME-BOUND STUDY, examining U.S. and European counterterrorism efforts from the September 11 attacks until June 2005, when I returned to federal government service. It does not include analysis of events that occurred after that period.

Of course, several relevant developments have unfolded in the United States and Europe since June 2005, including additional arrests and prosecutions of suspected terrorists, noteworthy legal changes, key judicial decisions, and both failed and successful terrorist attacks. Although these developments are certainly important, I believe that the underlying analysis and conclusions in this book remain both accurate and timely. Indeed, many recent events validate its arguments, particularly those regarding the growing European terrorist threat and the ongoing difficulties associated with prosecuting suspected terrorists on both sides of the Atlantic. Moreover, the similarities between U.S. and European counterterrorism efforts still receive little attention, even as both parties continue to employ similar approaches in several key areas.

In light of these facts, the recommendations outlined in the chapters that follow—which are intended as practical, workable solutions to the common problems that the U.S. and European governments face—remain applicable today. Note, however, that the views expressed in this book are my own and not necessarily those of the U.S. government.

Michael Jacobson
May 2006

Executive Summary

SINCE THE ATTACKS OF SEPTEMBER 11, 2001, MUCH attention has been devoted to the effectiveness of U.S. counterterrorism efforts, with particular focus on whether the government has improved its ability to prevent devastating terrorist attacks. The American public and media are especially concerned about the government's efforts to neutralize the terrorist threat emanating from the Middle East and from unidentified domestic cells. At the same time, the United States has traditionally viewed the terrorist threat in Europe, and the counterterrorism efforts of individual European countries, as secondary in importance.

This perspective may—and probably should—shift in the years to come. Europe has become one of the most important battlegrounds in the global fight against Islamic terrorism, and what happens there has a direct impact on U.S. national security. As the September 11 attacks illustrated, terrorists living and training freely in Europe, undisturbed by European security services, can pose the greatest danger to the United States.

When comparing U.S. and European counterterrorism efforts, observers on both sides of the Atlantic tend to emphasize the differences between the two approaches. Many Europeans believe that the United States has abandoned the rule of law and resorted to almost exclusively military means in its counterterrorism efforts. For their part, many Americans perceive Europe as being soft on terrorism and unwilling to take the tough measures necessary to confront the terrorist threat.

Lost amid this often-heated rhetoric are the significant commonalities between the United States and several European countries in the terrorism arena. In particular, the United States, Germany, and Britain have adopted certain similar approaches to combating terrorism and have often encountered the same difficulties. Most significantly, U.S., German, and British law enforcement authorities and prosecutors are now primarily responsible for preventing terrorist attacks, not merely bringing perpetrators to justice after the fact. As a result, law enforcement agencies are often made aware of domestic intelligence operations at a far earlier stage than in the past, and consequently are able to take action much sooner. In all three countries, authorities were able to assume this more proactive posture in part because of legislation passed in the wake of the September 11 attacks.

This paradigm shift was driven largely by the realization among law enforcement and intelligence officials that terrorism of the type perpetrated by al-Qaeda and its affiliates represents a new type of threat. Before September 11, when the potential consequences of terrorist attacks were deemed less devastating, authorities were willing to watch terrorist suspects for lengthy periods rather than apprehending them immediately, in an effort to determine the exact details of a given plot. Now, however, authorities realize that they can no longer afford to take that chance.

Despite this policy shift, the United States, Germany, and Britain have all struggled in their post–September 11 efforts to target and prosecute suspected terrorists via law enforcement methods. The factors contributing to these problems are similar in all three countries.

First, there is a great deal of pressure to disrupt terrorist cells much earlier than in the past, well before they begin to execute an attack. As a result, the governments in question often prosecute individuals based simply on a belief that they are involved in terrorist activity, even though the exact details of their intentions may be unknown or too difficult to prove in court.

Second, for a variety of reasons, it is often problematic to use intelligence information in the course of a prosecution. Hence, authorities often face the difficult question of whether improving the chances of a given prosecution is worth exposing a particular source or method.

Third, prosecutions are increasingly becoming an international endeavor. Terrorist suspects often travel or have ties to numerous countries, and the cooperation of many governments is required for a successful prosecution. Complicating this task is the fact that there are many cases in which certain governments do not want their cooperation made public.

Fourth, not all countries have laws that are well designed for prosecuting suspected terrorists. Gaps remain even in countries like the United States, Germany, and Britain, which have made significant legal changes since September 11. Such laws need to be frequently reviewed and updated as the terrorist threat changes and as warranted by other developments.

These problems are not easy to solve. It is difficult enough for the United States to resolve the thorny issues associated with its own efforts to prosecute suspected terrorists, let alone to work with Europeans in addressing challenges they have encountered. Yet, given the fact that U.S. national security depends in part on the effectiveness of European counterterrorism efforts, Washington must attempt to succeed on both fronts.

There are several ways in which U.S. policymakers can improve their efforts to work with European authorities on these issues:

1. **Focus on commonalities.** Washington should shift attention away from the differences between the U.S. and European approaches to terrorism and focus more on their shared methods and problems. This would be a vitally important step toward showing skeptical American and European audiences that their governments are not as far apart as has been publicly portrayed.

2. **Initiate strategic collaboration.** Washington should also push for greater collaboration with Europe in tackling the difficult strategic issues with which they both have struggled. For example, they could create a special commission to study relevant issues and push for needed changes. Ideally, this commission would include representatives of the United States, the European Union (EU), and individual EU member states. Washington and key EU countries should also expand their use of strategies that have proven effective and encourage the rest of the EU to adopt them as well. These strategies include aggressively prosecuting terrorist suspects for nonterrorism-related crimes, ramping up efforts to criminalize and prosecute "material support" activity, and making counterterrorism a higher priority for law enforcement agencies and prosecutors.

3. **Improve tactical cooperation.** Although tactical counterterrorism cooperation between the United States and Europe has been good since September 11, it could certainly be improved further. Given the increasing difficulty of prosecuting terrorist suspects without help from foreign governments, it is essential that all parties remove obstacles to international cooperation in the law enforcement and prosecutorial arenas. For Europe, this would involve ensuring adequate protection of classified information during the course of trials and lengthening sentences for terrorism convictions. For its part, the United States should consider removing the death penalty as an option for terrorism prosecutions in which international cooperation is needed, given the widespread antipathy toward capital punishment in Europe.

4. **Encourage the EU to play a greater role.** Although many are dismissive of the role the EU has played in the national security arena, it is crucial that the United States work closely not only with individual EU states, but also with the EU as an entity. Where possible, Washington should urge the EU to assume a greater role in European counterterrorism activities. The United States should also take advantage of the "bureaucratic peer pressure" prevalent in the EU by asking countries with strong counterterrorism capabilities to spur their weaker neighbors toward improvement.

The ongoing struggles experienced by policymakers and law enforcement authorities on both sides of the Atlantic also suggest a number of key counterterrorism measures that Washington can take independently of Europe:

1. **Consider legislative solutions to facilitate prosecution of suspected terrorists.** The U.S. government should consider whether there are legislative measures—including fundamental reform of the criminal justice system—that would allow it to effectively prosecute all suspected terrorists. Despite the heated public debate surrounding related issues such as the USA PATRIOT Act and the Guantanamo Bay detentions, no fundamental legislative overhaul has been proposed, whether due to the challenges inherent in it or to the implied perception that the system itself is sacrosanct. Even if it is ultimately decided that enacting this type of sweeping reform is not the right solution, considering—and publicly debating—major legislative solutions is essential. Accordingly, Washington should examine a wide range of legislative proposals to address counterterrorism shortcomings, both broad and more narrowly tailored.

2. **Remove politics from counterterrorism prosecutions.** To the extent that judges—and, even more so, juries—regard the government's counterterrorism efforts as politicized, Washington is likely to encounter great difficulty in bringing successful counterterrorism prosecutions. To address these issues, Washington should adopt two policies:

   ■ *Comment as little as possible publicly about counterterrorism cases until after conviction.* Indictments should be allowed to speak for themselves.

- *Be far more cautious in its use of counterterrorism statistics.* Policy-makers should take great care to ensure that such statistics are accurate and not exaggerated in any way. Moreover, while it is important to release statistics of this sort, trumpeting them publicly often gives them political overtones.

3. **Ensure that prosecutors are sufficiently independent from law enforcement.** Although Washington must find a way to maintain the close ties that developed between prosecutors and law enforcement in the wake of the September 11 attacks, it must also ensure that prosecutors are sufficiently independent to make objective judgments about the merits of a given case.

Through these and other important steps, the United States can help improve efforts to curb terrorist activities on both sides of the Atlantic. All such efforts are vital to U.S. national security, regardless of who is carrying them out—U.S. agencies, European authorities, or, ideally, both in concert.

Introduction

THIS STUDY FOCUSES ON THE ROLE OF U.S. COUNTER-terrorism efforts in law enforcement and prosecution since September 11, comparing them with similar efforts in Britain and Germany. We focus primarily on those law enforcement and prosecution entities in each country that play the most important role in counterterrorism, and not on agencies more tangentially involved.

In the United States, law enforcement and prosecution of counterterrorism are handled primarily by the Federal Bureau of Investigation (FBI) and the Justice Department. While many federal and state law enforcement agencies now play a larger role in counterterrorism than they did before September 11, the dominant agency in this arena remains the FBI, because of its size and jurisdiction. The FBI has 29,000 employees, with 56 offices in the United States and nearly 50 more overseas—easily dwarfing other law enforcement agencies in scope. The FBI also has the broadest jurisdiction of any of the federal law enforcement agencies, both in the counterterrorism arena and in other areas. The FBI has lead U.S. responsibility in investigating counterterrorism, and also has jurisdiction for investigating the illegal drug trade, kidnapping, white-collar crime, and counterintelligence, among other matters. In terms of counterterrorism prosecutions, federal prosecutions in the United States are conducted by the Justice Department, which consists not only of its main offices in Washington, but of 93 individual federal prosecutors' offices throughout the country.

In Britain, counterterrorism law enforcement operations are handled mainly by the Metropolitan Police of New Scotland Yard—which has both investigative and coordinating responsibility—and by the police "Special Branches." Each of Britain's 43 police constabularies has its own Special Branch, responsible for counterterrorism and other national security investigations. The Metropolitan Police and the various Special Branches all report to the Home Office, an agency roughly analogous to the U.S. Justice Department. Counterterrorism prosecutions in the United Kingdom are carried out by the Crown Prosecution Service, in conjunction with nongovernmental barristers.

1

In Germany, counterterrorism law enforcement operations are primarily the responsibility of the federation's 16 states, each with its own law enforcement agency (Landeskriminalamt, or LKA). The German federal law enforcement agency (Bundeskriminalamt, or BKA) also plays an important role in counterterrorism. Each state has its own Interior Ministry overseeing the local LKAs, while the federal Interior Ministry supervises the BKA. Counterterrorism cases are generally prosecuted by the federal prosecutor's office, which is responsible solely for national security matters, such as espionage and terrorism prosecutions. The federal prosecutor's office is under the purview of the federal Justice Ministry.

The terms "law enforcement" and "prosecutor" are used liberally throughout this monograph. Though these categories could include a wide variety of agencies beyond those listed above in each of these countries, they are generally used here to refer to the agencies most integrally involved in counterterrorism. There are, not surprisingly, some difficulties in making direct comparisons between the United States, Germany, and Britain in the counterterrorism arena. Probably the most important limitation in this regard is that the United States has a different domestic structure for countering terrorism than other Western democracies. In Britain, France, and Germany, for example, responsibility for gathering intelligence on terrorist threats and criminal investigations is shared by a domestic intelligence and law enforcement agency. The domestic intelligence agencies, such as MI-5 (or British Security Service) in the United Kingdom, the Direction de la Surveillance du Territoire (DST) in France, and the Bundesamt für Verfassungsschutz (BFV) in Germany, do not have the powers of arrest. The FBI, by contrast, has both criminal law enforcement and intelligence responsibilities in the counterterrorism arena.[1] This study will focus more on the FBI's law enforcement duties, and less on its intelligence responsibilities or capabilities. Other important differences between the U.S. and European systems make direct comparisons and recommendations difficult. For example, Britain, unlike the United States and Germany, is not a federal system; Germany, unlike the United States and Britain, operates under a civil law—and not a common law—system.[2]

This study focuses primarily on domestic aspects of the U.S., British, and German counterterrorism efforts, though there will be limited discussion about law enforcement agencies' cooperation and coordination with the foreign intelligence agencies—the Central Intelligence Agency (CIA) in the United States, the BND (Bundesnachrichtendienst) in Germany, and MI-6 (or Secret Intelligence Service) in Britain. In the case of the United States, where the FBI has responsibility for both domestic law enforcement and intelligence, this limited approach will largely mean exploring the relationship between the FBI's law enforcement and intelligence elements.

While this study compares U.S. counterterrorism efforts since September 11 with those of Western Europe, a review of every European country's efforts would have precluded in-depth research or analysis. Therefore, this study uses a "case study" approach, focusing on two European countries—Germany and Britain—as examples. Still, this monograph will touch on the efforts of other European countries, and will offer a brief assessment of the evolving role of the European Union (EU) in the counterterrorism arena. It may be argued that Britain, in particular, is not representative of broader European views, and is far more similar to the United States than any other European country, but similar arguments could be made for other European countries. Given that every European nation has its own culture, priorities, and history, it would be hard to identify one country whose counterterrorism efforts are perfectly representative of a "European" approach.

Since the study looks at the role of the criminal justice system in counterterrorism, an important part of the research was trying to understand how the subject countries' approaches were shaped by their underlying legal systems. It therefore made sense to consider a country with a civil law system, like Germany, and one with a common law system similar to that of the United States, like Britain. Conventional wisdom often holds that countries with very different legal systems can teach each other very little on criminal justice issues. The systems are so different, it is frequently argued, that comparisons and analogies between them are generally not useful. While direct analogies can indeed be difficult to make, this study aims to show that different underlying legal systems do not preclude noteworthy similarities, and that the United States and its European allies can learn important lessons from one another, and can collaborate to more effectively tackle problems we all face.

Notes

1. For a more thorough study of how the U.S. domestic intelligence structure compares with those of other Western democracies, see Peter Chalk, William Rosenau, *Confronting the Enemy Within: Security Intelligence, the Police, and Counterterrorism in Four*

Democracies (Santa Monica, Calif.: RAND, 2004). Available online (http://rand.org/pubs/monographs/2004/RAND_MG100.sum.pdf).

2. In civil law systems, comprehensive codes and statutes make up the body of law, and judicial decisions have little impact in shaping the law. In common law systems, on the other hand, while federal and state legislatures pass laws, courts play the most important role in shaping the law due to the concept of the "precedence" of legal decisions. Common law systems also use juries in both civil and criminal cases, while in civil law systems the judges always play this role. The United Kingdom and the United States have common law systems, while continental European, Latin American, and many other countries have civil law systems. Judge Peter Messitte, "Common Law vs. Civil Law Systems," *Issues of Democracy* 4, no. 2 (U.S. Information Agency, December 1999); available online (http://usinfo.state.gov/journals/itdhr/0999/ijde/ijde0999.pdf).

The Importance of European Counterterrorism to U.S. National Security

SINCE THE SEPTEMBER 11 ATTACKS, THERE HAS BEEN considerable focus in the United States on the effectiveness of the government's counterterrorism efforts, particularly on whether the United States has improved its capability to prevent devastating terrorist attacks. The American public and media have been most concerned about their government's ability to neutralize the terrorist threat emanating from the Middle East, and from unidentified cells within the United States. European counterterrorism efforts, on the other hand, have often been viewed as secondary in importance. This perspective may, and should, shift in the years to come. Europe has become one of the most important battlegrounds in the global fight against Islamic terrorism, and what is happening in Europe can have—and already has had—a direct impact on U.S. national security. Europe's battleground status should not concern only Europeans; experts agree that many of the terrorists living and training in Europe are likely plotting attacks against U.S. targets, in addition to European ones. As the September 11 attacks illustrated most vividly, terrorists based in Europe, undisturbed by European security agencies, may pose the greatest threat to U.S. security.

What makes this issue one of even higher importance to the United States is that the counterterrorism efforts of European Union (EU) member states remain uneven. While some EU countries take the terrorism threat seriously and have strong intelligence and law enforcement capabilities, not all do. Moreover, cooperation and coordination on counterterrorism within Europe is problematic—a particularly dangerous vulnerability given the ease of movement and travel across EU boundaries. These vulnerabilities should be of great concern not only to Europeans themselves, but to U.S. policymakers as well. Consequently, an assessment of European countries' post–September 11 counterterrorism efforts—in this case focusing on Germany and Britain—is much more than an academic exercise.

Europe As Battleground

The March 11, 2004, Madrid bombings, which killed 191 people, provided the first striking evidence of an Islamist terrorist problem in Europe after

September 11. Over the past several years, suspected terrorist plotters have also been arrested in almost every Western European country, including Italy, Britain, Germany, Spain, Holland, and Belgium. Despite the arrests, European counterterrorism experts believe that there may still be more than 1,000 suspected terrorists currently living and operating in Europe. Dutch security officials, for example, believe they know of approximately 150 people with both connections to terrorist organizations and the ability to conduct terrorist operations against Holland.[1] One observer has noted that while Europe was previously viewed as a "relative backwater in the war on terror, Europe is now in the frontline."[2]

Though the Madrid attack was the first truly spectacular terrorist operation in Europe following September 11, a much smaller attack later in 2004 may more accurately illustrate the threat many European countries face. In November of that year an Islamist activist murdered Theo Van Gogh, a Dutch filmmaker who had recently made a controversial film criticizing the treatment of Muslim women.[3] Dutch police have since arrested the alleged perpetrator, Muhammad Bouyeri, and his associates, who reportedly have ties to the al-Qaeda-linked Moroccan Islamic Combatant Group. The attack is important because the alleged perpetrator and his associates are not foreign jihadists, but Dutch citizens raised in Holland. Thus, the Van Gogh attack illustrates a disturbing new trend in Europe, that of young European-born Muslims who have turned to radical Islam as a consequence of alienation and disenfranchisement from European society. Holland is not the only western European country to have a "parallel society" of Muslims, many of whom are born in Europe and are EU citizens, but remain poorly integrated into mainstream life. As Robert Leiken writes, "The murder of filmmaker Theo Van Gogh by a Dutch Muslim of Moroccan descent served notice for a new generation of mujahideen born and bred in Europe and the object of focused al-Qaeda post-9-11 and post-Iraq recruitment."[4]

Britain faces a particularly serious terrorist threat; many experts believe the United Kingdom is the second highest priority target for Islamist terrorists, after the United States.[5] During an early 2005 British parliamentary debate over a proposal to establish "control orders" (a form of far-reaching security measures) for suspected terrorists, it became clear just how serious the British security officials believe the terrorist threat to be. Despite widespread criticism, Prime Minister Tony Blair refused to grant many of the compromises demanded by the opposition, arguing that police and security services had advised him not to dilute the laws. As he noted, "Should any terrorist attack occur, there will not be a debate about civil liberties; there will be a debate about the advice that the government received, and about whether they followed it."[6] According to Sir John Stevens, the former chief of New Scotland Yard, the terrorist threat was so serious that there were "at least 100 Osama bin Laden-trained terrorists walking Britain's streets," adding that he believed the number to be closer to 200.[7] In addition to demonstrating the gravity of the threat, Stevens's comments also illustrate how the British perception of the threat has changed in recent years. In the immediate wake of September 11, UK officials believed that the threat to Britain was largely an external one—that is, coming from non-British citizens. For this reason, Parliament passed legislation containing a provision allowing indefinite detention of foreign nationals; British citizens were not considered a likely problem. But in the past few years, the British government has come to realize that the threat is also very much an internal one. Indeed, a small number of British Muslims have been drawn into extremism, and have even been pulled into the operational realm.[8]

Several factors have contributed to the rapid rise of Islamic fundamentalism in Britain. In the United Kingdom, there is an increasing number of second and third generation British Muslims—most from South Asia—who are alienated from mainstream British society. This demographic trend is amplified by the number of already radical Muslims who have moved to Britain over the past decade to take advantage of the UK's liberal political asylum laws. Britain's immigration policies have also allowed communities to import Muslim imams from abroad quite easily, many of whom preach extremist ideologies. This "explosive combination" of factors has resulted in an environment in which "fundamentalist ideology is mainstream ideology."[9]

Some of the extremists who have immigrated to Britain are from North Africa. In fact, the largest number of North Africans arrested since September 11 were detained on British soil. Some observers believe that this pattern demonstrates a shift in immigration patterns for North Africans, who have historically preferred France to Britain, but who may now be finding the security regime in France overly harsh. (Until recently, the British were far more reluctant than the French to crack down on extremism.[10]) Whatever the reason for the growing radicalization of this group, it is clear that there are now many native-born British Muslims who have become radicalized while living in Britain. For example, two British citizens (one of whom was native born) were involved in a May 2003 suicide attack in Israel.[11] Two other well-publicized examples have also illustrated this relatively new phenomenon. Saajid Badat, a twenty-five-year-old British-born associate of shoe bomber Richard Reid, likely became radicalized in the late 1990s at a South London mosque. He then spent two years at an al-Qaeda training camp in Afghanistan. Senior Metropolitan police official Peter Clarke discussed Badat's radicalization after his guilty plea for conspiracy to blow up an aircraft: "We must ask how a young British man was transformed from an intelligent, articulate person who was well respected into a person who has pleaded guilty to one of the most serious crimes that you can think of."[12]

The case of Ahmed Omar Saeed Sheikh offers an even more striking and surprising example of a young British Muslim who chose the path of extremism. Sheikh was born in London in 1973 to parents who had arrived from Pakistan in the late 1960s. His father was a successful businessman, and Sheikh was educated at exclusive British private schools, including the London School of Economics, where he studied math and statistics before dropping out. At some point, Sheikh became involved with extremist elements, joining the Pakistani terrorist group Harkat-ul-Mujahedin (HUM), and eventually making his way to the al-Qaeda camps in Afghanistan.[13] In an interview with a Pakistani magazine, Sheikh acknowledged that while in Afghanistan he met several times with Osama bin Laden.[14] After joining the HUM, Sheikh participated in an attempted kidnapping of Western tourists in Pakistan, an operation designed to secure the release of a HUM member who had been imprisoned by the Pakistani government. During the course of the operation, Sheikh was captured by police and imprisoned. Demonstrating how valuable a member Sheikh had become, the HUM conducted two subsequent operations designed to free Sheikh, including a 1999 aircraft hijacking through which the terrorist group successfully negotiated the release of Sheikh and one other HUM member. Once free from prison, Sheikh resumed his terrorist activities, allegedly participating in the murder of *Wall Street Journal* reporter Daniel Pearl.[15] Sheikh was convicted by a Pakistani court of this crime, and sentenced to death. He is currently appealing his conviction.[16]

Though Germany's internal threat may not be as serious as that facing Britain or France, the head of counterterrorism for the German federal police has said, "Germany cannot be ruled out as a target." In fact, the Germans believe that they have prevented four or five domestic terrorist attacks since September 11.[17] The country has increased in appeal as a target of Islamic terrorists because of its military cooperation with the United States in Afghanistan, and because of Germany's increasingly aggressive counter-terrorism efforts. Consequently, there have been at least several examples of Islamic groups targeting German interests directly, including at least two attacks on German troops in Afghanistan, and an attack on German tourists in Tunisia. More likely, perhaps, than an attack on German targets per se is an attack on U.S., British, or Israeli interests located in Germany. A number of groups operating within Germany could conduct such an operation. For example, Ansar al-Islam, an Iraqi terrorist group funded in part by al-Qaeda, has a particularly strong presence in Germany and has been using the country both as a base to conduct internal attacks and as a recruitment ground for young Muslims it can direct to fight in Iraq. For example, three members of an Ansar cell with "close contact to the highest leadership circles" of the organization were arrested in December 2004. German officials believe that they were planning to assassinate interim Iraqi Prime Minister Ayad Allawi during his visit to Germany. In December 2003, German authorities arrested an individual in Munich whom they accused of facilitating the travel of approximately a dozen fighters to Iraq, and also of helping injured Ansar members return to Europe for medical treatment. Germany believes that between ten and fifty individuals from Bavaria alone have gone to Iraq to aid the insurgency.[18]

According to German estimates, the number of individuals active in radical Islamist organizations in Germany slightly increased during 2003, and by 2004 stood at almost 32,000.[19] Among these 32,000 are members of al-Qaeda's networks, including Abu Musab al-Zarqawi's terrorist group. By and large, most of these groups' activities in Germany focus on providing logistical support and militant recruitment, not actual operational planning. There are notable exceptions, however. Germany believes that Zarqawi instructed his network to plan attacks on Jewish and Israeli facilities in Germany. In 2002, German authorities disrupted this plot, arresting twelve members of the network.[20] In late January 2005, German authorities arrested two suspected al-Qaeda members, charging them with belonging to a foreign terrorist organization. German officials allege that the men were not only planning suicide bombings in Iraq, but had also planned to purchase a small amount of enriched uranium.[21] According to the German internal security service, the Muslim Brotherhood, Hamas, and Hizballah are also active in Germany.[22]

That these groups were all operating in Germany was a revelation to German officials. Before September 11, the general perception in Germany was that there was not much radical Islamist activity in the country, whose foreign residents are mostly Turkish nationals who moved to Germany as "guest workers," beginning in the 1960s. The conventional wisdom at the time was that Turks, whose home country is a secular Muslim state, tended not to become radicalized.[23] Perhaps owing to the dominance of Turkish immigration, there was less focus in Germany on non-Turkish nationals from the Middle East who had settled there.

In fact, the driving force behind the increased radicalization in Germany has been the immigration of radical Muslims from the Arab world. Germany has hosted many extremist imams trained in the Middle East and then sent to preach in Germany.[24] These imams have played an important role in the radicalization of German Muslim communities, in some cases successfully radicalizing elements of the Turkish population. Many German Turks are out of work and not well integrated into German society—an unfortunate fact that is partly attributable to German immigration laws. (Most Turks living in Germany are not German citizens because until 1999 being born in Germany did not qualify one for citizenship.[25]) As a result, Germany's Turkish residents may feel more vulnerable and become, in some cases, receptive to radical ideologies.[26]

Europe is likely to maintain its status on the front lines of global terrorism for the foreseeable future. In fact, many observers believe the terrorist threat in Europe will only increase in the coming years. The Muslim population in Europe, which currently numbers approximately twenty million, is increasing at a much faster rate than the rest of the European population. As the Muslim community in Europe increases, integration may become even more difficult—further alienating the Muslim communities. There is also the danger of an anti-Muslim backlash in some Western countries, a regrettable phenomenon that will also undermine governmental efforts toward integration. Underscoring the importance of European Muslims in the global ideological struggle, French scholar Gilles Kepel wrote in his most recent book that "the war for Muslim minds around the world may turn on the outcome" of the European governments' efforts to integrate the growing and increasingly radical Muslim populations in Europe.[27]

Al-Qaeda's Expanded Target List

Increased radicalization and disenchantment of Muslim youths in Europe is only one of several factors behind the increased terrorist threat there. Europe's status as a terrorism battleground is heightened by al-Qaeda's apparent decision to broaden its target list beyond the United States and across the Western world.[28] In a November 2002 audiotape, an individual believed to be Osama bin Laden specifically identified as acceptable targets European countries such as Germany, France, Italy, and Britain, as well as Canada and Australia. Bin Laden's supporters have heeded his call, conducting or attempting attacks on numerous European targets. These have included trains in Madrid, German citizens in Tunisia, French oil tankers off the Yemeni coast, and British targets in Turkey. While American targets undoubtedly remain a high priority, the United States is no longer alone atop the target list.[29] As Jonathan Stevenson writes, "Broadly construed, Europe may be al-Qaeda's highest-value 'field of jihad' other than the United States."[30]

Before September 11, al-Qaeda and bin Laden were focused solely on attacking the United States and American interests. Targets included U.S. embassies in Kenya and Tanzania, the USS *Cole* and USS *The Sullivans* in Yemen, and, of course, the Pentagon and World Trade Center. The September 11 attacks were the culmination of a series of increasingly violent al-Qaeda attacks on U.S. targets and represented the successful redirection of Sunni extremist groups' focus from their own governments to the United States. Before the rise of al-Qaeda, for example, Algerian Sunni extremist groups were intent on attacking the Algerian government, while like-minded Egyptian groups were focused on overthrowing the Egyptian regime.[31] Bin Laden believed this to be a wrongheaded strategy, arguing that attacks against the United States were more potent, America being the "head of the snake." [32]

Terrorists in Europe Targeting U.S. Interests

September 11 was proof positive that terrorist activity in Europe can have an immediate and catastrophic impact on the United States. The four core members of the September 11 conspiracy's "Hamburg cell," as they are now known, spent years in that German city. They were part of a group of radical Muslims who met often to discuss and share anti-American sentiments. One of the hijackers' Hamburg associates, Muhammad Haydar Zammar, reportedly took credit for influencing the cell members, and encouraging them to participate in jihad. Zammar was a prominent figure in the German Muslim community, and U.S. and German intelligence agencies were well aware of him by the late 1990s.[33] However, prior to September 11, significant legal barriers restricted Germany's ability to target Islamic fundamentalism. The 9-11 Commission concluded that al-Qaeda was able to exploit "relatively lax internal environments in Western countries, especially Germany."[34]

While September 11 is the most extreme example of how events in Europe can impact the United States, it is far from the only one. In fact, as one al-Qaeda expert testified, "Every single attack carried out or attempted by al-Qaeda throughout the world has some link to Europe, even prior to September 11."[35] This sentiment was echoed by noted al-Qaeda expert Peter Bergen during congressional testimony, when he said, "The greatest threat to the United States from al-Qaeda, its affiliated groups, or those animated by al-Qaeda's ideology emanates from Europe." Future attacks against U.S. interests are, in Bergen's view, "likely to have a European connection."[36] There are numerous examples since September 11 of suspected terrorists arrested in Europe on suspicion of plotting to attack U.S. interests—both in Europe and elsewhere. In March 2005, a French court convicted six Islamic extremists of conspiring to carry out a suicide bombing against the U.S. embassy in Paris. They were sentenced to prison terms of between three-and-a-half and ten years. The group of young men—most were in their twenties and thirties—included both immigrants from North Africa and Muslim converts. Several of their other associates, including the person who had apparently been selected as the suicide bomber, had earlier been convicted of terrorism charges in Belgium and Holland. The Paris embassy plot underscores that the threat to the United States in Europe is a pan-European one, and is not restricted to one country. Although the attack was to take place in France, this group also had cells in Belgium and Holland, according to prosecutors. In addition, the plotters spent time in radical mosques in Britain, where they were taught by Abu Qatada, an extremist imam detained by the British after September 11.[37]

Recent events in Europe have demonstrated that jihadists in Europe continue to pose a great potential danger not only to U.S. interests in Europe, but to the territorial United States as well. For example, in August 2004, British authorities arrested eight terrorist suspects, charging them with planning an attack using "radioactive materials, toxic gases, chemicals, and/or explosives." One of the suspects, Dhiren Barot, was accused by Britain of having "reconnaissance plans" of buildings in New York and Washington, including the Citigroup building, the New York Stock Exchange, and the International Monetary Fund headquarters in Washington. Barot and a second person, Nadeem Tarmohammed, were charged with having reconnaissance plans for the Prudential building in New York as well. They were charged under a provision of Britain's 2000 Terrorism Act making it a crime to have documents useful to a person planning to commit a terrorist act.[38] FBI officials subsequently announced they were trying to retrace Barot's steps because he spent time in New Jersey in 2000 and 2001. The bureau stated that it was focused particularly on determining whether any of Barot's associates remained in the area.[39]

In addition to the threat of traditional terrorist attacks by European Muslims, it now appears that many young Muslims in Europe are being recruited to fight in the insurgency in Iraq. Ansar al-Islam, according to European intelligence officials, operates a large-scale recruiting network in Europe for this purpose. In 2003, Italian police arrested a dozen suspected Ansar members, alleging that they had smuggled approximately two hundred people into Iraq from Europe. These arrests led investigators to Ansar members in other European countries, including Sweden, Britain, and Germany.[40] European jihadists who have fought in Iraq may represent a particularly serious future threat to U.S. and European national security. As the State Department observed in its "Country Report on Terrorism 2004," foreign jihadists are attempting to transform Iraq into this generation's Afghanistan, a "melting pot for jihadists from around the world, a training ground, and an indoctrination center."[41] The end result may be that many of these jihadists return to their home countries more experienced, better trained, and perhaps more inspired to commit violence. They may then form their own terrorist cells, or help improve the capabilities of groups already in place.

J. Cofer Black, the former State Department Coordinator for Counterterrorism, has agreed that insurgency experience has made jihadists far more dangerous, noting that "not so many have to get past you when they are trained so well in explosives." Black predicted that Iraq-experienced jihadists will have a dramatic effect on Europeans and Americans: "The quality of our lives will change to a certain extent, as measures previously considered needed (only) in forward areas will increasingly be ... adopted in our home countries." Roger Cressey, former deputy counterterrorism coordinator for the White House, assessed these jihadists' threat from a different angle. He argued that they are now used to "being hunted in a much more aggressive fashion than by law enforcement" and, as a result, have developed skills to elude detection that will make them difficult to track or detain if they leave Iraq.[42] As Black implied, these developments could have serious ramifications for the security of the continental United States. Many current insurgents in Iraq are citizens of European countries, and as such can enter the United States under the Visa Waiver Program. Many also speak English, have experience living in Western countries, and are computer savvy.[43]

Remaining Problems with European Counterterrorism Efforts

The mounting terrorist threat from groups based in Europe is caused in part by unsatisfactory counterterrorism measures across the EU. While some European countries such as Germany and Britain have been aggressive since September 11 in improving their counterterrorism capabilities, many other European countries have not made comparable changes. In fact, senior U.S. administration officials have been publicly critical at times of EU counterterrorism efforts. In testimony before the Senate Foreign Relations Committee in March 2004, Cofer Black pointed out that although Europe has been a "solid partner" in the war on terrorism, "significant deficiencies remain" in its counterterrorism efforts. Black cited a wide array of problems, including inadequate counterterrorism legislation; difficulties in prosecuting terrorist suspects; strict privacy laws that can complicate counterterrorism investigations; lax sentencing guidelines; varying immigration policies among EU member states; and differing perspectives on what constitutes legitimate political or charitable activity, as opposed to terrorism support.[44] According to him, these deficiencies arise at both the member state and pan-European level.

At the member state level, the problems are attributable both to deficiencies in capability and to a lack of interest in counterterrorism. Many EU members simply do not have an adequate law enforcement or intelligence capability to handle a major terrorist threat.[45] Moreover, while Germany and Britain may now better appreciate the terrorism threat, other European countries are less cognizant of the danger and regard it primarily as a thorn in the side of the United States. For example, the Scandinavian countries, according to one expert, view terrorism as "something exotic, down there in the South."[46] According to a senior EU official, of the twenty-five EU member states, probably fewer than ten have a real interest in counterterrorism.[47]

The Netherlands is often cited as an example of a country that has had difficulties coping with an increased internal terrorist threat, a problem conceded even by Dutch security officials. Dutch counterterrorism officials have noted that while they are aware of approximately 150 suspected terrorists, the country lacks the resources to closely monitor all of them. In the case of alleged Van Gogh assailant Muhammad Bouyeri, this lack of resources may have had serious consequences. Dutch officials acknowledge that they were aware of Bouyeri's extremist sympathies prior to his alleged actions, but assessed him as an unlikely terrorism candidate.[48] The Dutch have also had trouble over the past several years in their attempts to prosecute terrorist suspects. A Netherlands court, for example, acquitted Samir Azzouz, an eighteen-year-old Dutch Muslim charged with "making preparations for terrorist attacks." Law enforcement authorities believed that Azzouz was a member of the so-called "Hofstad" group, which included Bouyeri and his associates. Azzouz was charged after the police raided his house and discovered possible targeting information on various Dutch facilities, including the Amsterdam airport, a nuclear power plant, and the lower house of Parliament. In acquitting Azzouz, the court found that there was not enough evidence to convict him of the terrorism-related charges, though he was convicted of illegal arms possession.[49]

There have been other unsuccessful cases in the Netherlands in which the proceedings against terrorist suspects have ended before reaching the trial stage. In October 2003, Dutch police detained four individuals who were identified by Spanish police in an unrelated raid. According to the *Los Angeles Times*, one of the suspects was in possession of bombmaking materials, and Spain warned the Netherlands of a "plot in the works." Nevertheless, Dutch prosecutors released the four for lack of evidence. The *Los Angeles Times* article suggests that this situation is hardly atypical for the Dutch, and that European police agencies have intercepted communications in which terrorist suspects are "scoffing" at the laxness of the Netherlands' terrorism-related laws.[50]

Dutch commitment to prosecuting suspected terrorists might again be tested in the near future. The government is preparing to prosecute additional members of the Hofstad group, and observers have noted that the outcome in the Azzouz case "does not bode well" for the government's proceedings against the other alleged members of his group.[51] The Dutch government recently addressed the problem, passing a terrorism bill that gives law enforcement far more powers—though this bill still requires parliamentary approval as of this writing. Even if the bill passes, however, its effectiveness will be determined by how aggressively Dutch law enforcement agencies and prosecutors take advantage of their increased power.[52] Given the ease of travel throughout Europe, these issues should concern not only the Dutch, but other European countries and the United States as well.

In addition to gaps at the member state level, internal European cooperation and coordination on counterterrorism remain problematic. French terrorism investigator Jean-Louis Bruguiere has complained that information sharing in Europe is often laborious, when action is required "in real time." Other experts have noted that intelligence agencies are still hesitant to share information with their EU counterparts, because of concerns about protecting sources.[53] According to Bruguiere, entities such as Europol, the EU-wide police agency, had not yet reached their full potential.[54] The Madrid bombings, according to Antonio Vitorino, the former EU commissioner for justice and home affairs, were a "wake-up call" that illustrated the need to fix "old rivalries" among European intelligence and law enforcement services. Vitorino conceded, however, that "we cannot fix this overnight" and that "the sharing of intelligence among member states is still far from desirable."[55]

Europe's internal information sharing problems are particularly troubling given the ease of movement and travel across the European Union. With few internal borders, once an individual has made it into one member country, he can freely travel to most others in the union. Consequently, Europe's counterterrorism efforts are, to some extent, only as good as its weakest link. Consider the wide-ranging travels throughout Europe of Rabei Osman Sayed Ahmed, an Egyptian radical arrested by Italian authorities in June 2004. The *Washington Post* reported that Ahmed, who was first detained by the Germans in 1999 and placed in a camp for asylum seekers, left the camp several weeks prior to the September 11 attacks. From then until his arrest, according to the *Washington Post*, Ahmed allegedly attended fundamentalist mosques, recruited for suicide missions, and played a "key role" in planning the Madrid attacks. Ahmed was able to engage in these activities despite being reportedly tracked by at least three separate European countries. One personal conversation intercepted by Italian authorities revealed his confidence in being able to travel unconcerned and free throughout Europe: "I know who they are, but they don't know who I am. You confuse them, they won't know where you came from... You're clandestine, but you move around with no problem."[56]

Intelligence cooperation among EU states is even more essential when we consider that many terrorist cells are not based in one specific European country; rather, they tend to be scattered across the continent. Regardless of the effectiveness of any individual EU state, counterterrorism efforts cannot succeed without assistance and coordination from other member states. Several notable examples help illustrate how a terrorist network can operate across multiple EU countries and why this geographic feature is such a serious challenge for any state to handle individually.

Six individuals were convicted in 2005 of plotting to blow up the U.S. embassy in Paris. According to the prosecutors, the convicted six, and their associates, had set up covert cells in multiple countries, including France, Belgium, and the Netherlands. Many of the plotters had also spent considerable time in Britain. When France decided soon after September 11 to disrupt the cell, French authorities had to secure the cooperation of law enforcement counterparts in Belgium, the Netherlands, and Spain, who arrested the suspect present in their respective countries. Ultimately, in addition to the six people convicted in France, other cell members were prosecuted in the Netherlands and Belgium.[57]

During an arrest in Paris in late 2002, police found several suspicious items in the apartment of the suspects, including a chemical and biological warfare suit and some liquid chemicals. French authorities subsequently arrested twenty-five people, some of whom they believed had trained in Afghanistan. During their investigation, the French also discovered some connections to individuals in Britain, which information they passed to British authorities. Acting on this tip, UK officials conducted multiple raids throughout the country. Computer disks seized during one of the British searches pointed to additional connections in Spain. After receiving this information from Britain, Spanish authorities conducted their own raids, in which sixteen more suspects were arrested. Italy also became involved after finding in a Verona apartment the names of some of the British suspects.[58]

While the above two transnational terrorist networks were disrupted before they were able to strike, European counterterrorism has not always been so successful. European authorities now attribute a number of the post–September 11 attacks to a group believed to be increasingly operating across national boundaries. The Moroccan Islamic Combatant

Group, loosely tied to al-Qaeda, has been linked to attacks in Madrid, Casablanca, and the Netherlands. Counterterrorism officials now regard this group as much larger and more dangerous than they had previously realized; unfortunately, they have as yet been unable to locate many of the group's leaders, despite fairly intensive efforts.[59] Without better cooperation and coordination among European security services, it is unlikely that the Europeans will have great success in combating such loose extremist networks.

Although the Madrid attack was the first spectacular post–September 11 evidence of a terrorist threat in Europe, it did not have as much of an impact elsewhere in Europe—either at the member state or pan-European level—as might be expected. Many European countries viewed the Madrid attack as a primarily Spanish problem.[60] Spain, after all, had always been a focus of al-Qaeda's attention, as it contains land that was once part of the Islamic caliphate. Unlike many European countries, Spain also provided military assistance to the United States in Iraq. In fact, in March 2003, an al-Qaeda member warned Spain to stay out of Iraq, noting, "The wound of the occupation of Andalusia [Spain] has not healed."[61]

The murder of Theo Van Gogh in the Netherlands appears to have been a far more powerful wake-up call for many European countries. The Netherlands considered itself safe from terrorist attacks, given its tolerance toward minorities. In fact, as one observer noted, "No Western country had gone further than the Netherlands in accommodating its Muslim immigrants."[62] The attack and subsequent mosque burning hit home not only in the Netherlands, but also in other European countries with Muslim populations that were seemingly less well integrated. The attack sparked particular concern in Germany, which has a sizeable and fairly segregated Muslim population, largely Turkish. Dieter Wiefelspütz of Germany's Social Democratic Party put it bluntly, stating, "Holland is everywhere," in reference to the Van Gogh attack.[63] In fact, a poll conducted two weeks after the attack found that 57 percent of Germans believed that there was a "very high risk" that such an attack would also occur in Germany.[64] The topic of "parallel societies" had long been taboo in Germany, but after the attack it became acceptable for politicians to discuss more openly the problem, and potential solutions.[65] As of this writing, however, it is still far too early to judge the extent to which the Van Gogh attack will prompt serious reform and counterterrorism improvements both in the European member states and at the pan-European level.

Progress in European Counterterrorism Efforts

In theory, the European Union is the governmental body best positioned to address Europe's counterterrorism deficiencies, both at the member state and pan-European levels. However, while the union has gradually assumed a greater role in European counterterrorism efforts since September 11—a trend that appears likely to continue—it still plays only a limited and narrow role in European counterterrorism efforts overall. Since September 11, the European Union has made a greater effort to assume a role in the justice and home affairs arena, with some success. The most widely publicized development was the creation of a European counterterrorism "czar" in May 2004, in the wake of the Madrid train bombings. Appointed to this position was Gijs De Vries, a former Dutch interior minister and member of the European Parliament. De Vries was charged with coordinating the development of EU-wide counterterrorism policy.

Before September 11 the European Union played almost no role in criminal justice matters, a category that included counterterrorism. The 1992 treaty establishing the union created three separate areas—or "pillars"—for EU policy. The union's primary authority at setting policy fell under the first pillar, which covers economic, social, and environmental issues. The European Union's power was slightly more limited in the second pillar, which included foreign policy and military matters. The third pillar covered "justice and home affairs" matters, including counterterrorism, and the union's authority in this arena was far more limited than under the other two. Member states tended to regard the third pillar as highly sensitive, with national sovereignty implications, as it involved police and intelligence matters; they were unwilling to cede power in this arena to the EU.[66]

While the appointment of De Vries was the most publicized EU counterterrorism accomplishment since September 11, probably the most important development to date has been the creation of a European Arrest Warrant (EAW), which is intended to help member states combine law enforcement efforts across national borders, using common definitions and procedures. In the past, the issue of "dual criminality" has led to many highly public extradition battles between EU member states. Under this old principle, member states would extradite someone only if the alleged matter was a crime both in the state sending the extradition request and in the recipient state.[67] The EAW law—which is now the law in every EU member state but Italy—was intended to replace this extradition system. When faced with an EAW, a judge is supposed to grant extradition requests, with minimal review, regardless of whether the extraditing state's charge is considered a crime in the judge's state.[68] The EAW law appears to be already having a salutary impact on law enforcement, and has been used successfully in a number of cases. For example, Britain received and successfully processed approximately fifteen requests in the first three months after the law was passed.[69] Germany has also successfully used this new law in a number of cases, although the defendant in one case contested the legality of his expulsion. This case is currently pending before the German Constitutional Court.[70] The European Commission released an evaluation report in February 2005, declaring that the EAW had "broadly achieved its objectives."[71]

The most prominent use to date of an EAW was in the case of Youssef Belhadj, a suspected al-Qaeda spokesman implicated in the Madrid train bombings. Belhadj was arrested by Belgian authorities in response to an EAW issued by the Spanish government. Belhadj lost his challenge of the legality of the EAW, and was deported to Spain.[72] The EAW still faces some obstacles, however, before it can be considered a proper success. The European Commission has identified a number of problems in its evaluation, which have impeded the development of the EAW. For example, some member states have placed their own limitations on the application of the EAW, which may ultimately reduce its effectiveness.[73] Similarly, the European Union has debated whether to establish a European evidentiary warrant, which would allow a judge in one member state to obtain evidence in another member state for use in a criminal proceeding. Many observers believe that the union is likely to pass the evidentiary warrant in the near future.[74] The European Constitutional Treaty may also have an impact in this area, assuming that it is eventually ratified by the member states. The draft constitution would abolish the pillar structure, presumably allowing the European Union greater legislative freedom in the justice and home affairs arena.

Despite the many positive changes made since September 11, the European Union still plays a limited and narrow role in overall European counterterrorism efforts. While the EU has assumed some control in the legislative and policy arenas, it is not involved to any real extent in day-to-day counterterrorism matters. European intelligence and police work is still performed by the member states, and cooperation on counterterrorism matters between member states is done through either a bilateral or multilateral process—not through the EU. This situation appears unlikely to change in the near future. For example, during the debate over the European constitution, there arose a proposal to create a European public prosecutor. Such a position would greatly enhance the EU's involvement in daily criminal justice matters, but the proposal was quickly shot down. Observers regard it unlikely to be passed in the next decade, as it would too greatly infringe on national sovereignty.[75] Moreover, Europol and Eurojust, established by the EU to improve collaboration and cooperation between European police agencies and judges, respectively, have little actual authority to fulfill their mission. Europol, for example, can only cooperate on the "nonoperational" aspects of law enforcement, and is still without a permanent director.[76] Finally, the appointment of De Vries as counterterrorism czar appears to have had little impact at this point in centralizing Europe's counterterrorism efforts.[77] He has little in the way of concrete powers, and his responsibilities remain poorly defined.[78]

Notes

1. Michael Isikoff and Mark Hosenball, "Terror Watch: On the Loose," *Newsweek*, March 16, 2005.

2. Anthony Barnet, Jason Burke, and Zoe Smith, "Terror Cells Regroup—and Now Their Target Is Europe," *The Observer* (London), January 11, 2004.

3. "Al-Qaeda's New Front," *Frontline*, Public Broadcasting System, January 26, 2005. Available online (www.pbs.org/wgbh/pages/frontline/shows/front/map/nl.html).

4. Robert S. Leiken, "Europe's Mujahideen: Where Mass Immigration Meets Global Terrorism" (Washington, D.C.: Center for Immigration Studies, April 2005). Available online (www.cis.org/articles/2005/back405.html).

5. Jonathan Stevenson, "Counter-terrorism: Containment and Beyond," *Adelphi Paper* no. 367 (Washington, D.C.: International Institute for Strategic Studies, 2004), p. 52.

6. Alan Cowell, "Blair Rejects Demands for Milder Laws to Control Terror Suspects," *New York Times*, March 10, 2005. The full text of Blair's March 9, 2005, remarks to the House of Commons is available online (www.publications.parliament.uk/pa/cm200405/cmhansrd/cm050309/debtext/50309-03.htm).

7. Isikoff and Hosenball, "Terror Watch."

8. Peter Clarke (Senior Metropolitan police official), interview by author, January 2005.

9. Many of the Afghan Arabs moved to Britain after the war in Afghanistan ended in 1989. Some of them had first attempted to return to their home countries, but were

rejected. Robert S. Leiken, *Bearers of Global Jihad? Immigration and National Security After September 11* (Washington, D.C.: Nixon Center, 2004), p. 76.

10. Stevenson, "Counter-terrorism," p. 77.

11. Ibid.

12. Jason Bennetto, "British-Born Muslim Admits Plot to Blow Up Airliner," *Independent* (London), March 1, 2005.

13. Sajjan M. Gohel, *The Activities of Ahmed Omar Saeed Sheikh: An Example of the New Problem* (London: Asia-Pacific Foundation, February 24, 2005); Attorney General John Ashcroft (in speech given at State Department press conference announcing the indictment of Omar Saeed Ahmed Sheikh), March 14, 2002 (available online at www.state.gov/p/sa/rls/rm/8784.htm).

14. "Alleged Daniel Pearl Killer Says Met Bin Laden Twice: Report," Agence France Presse, April 19, 2005.

15. Gohel, "The Activities of Ahmed Omar Saeed Sheikh"; Ashcroft, press conference. Sheikh was indicted in March 2002 by the United States for his role in the kidnapping and murder of Pearl. He was also indicted earlier by a grand jury for his role in kidnapping an American in India in 1994.

16. See "Alleged Daniel Pearl Killer."

17. Juergen Maurer (in speech to German-American lawyers society), January 2005.

18. Craig Whitlock, "In Europe, New Force for Recruiting Radicals: Ansar al-Islam Emerges As Primary Extremist Group Funneling Fighters into Iraq," *Washington Post*, February 18, 2005.

19. *Bundesverfassungsschutzbericht* (BFV; Federal Constitution Protection Report), 2004.

20. BFV, 2003.

21. Matthew Schofield, "2 Suspected Terrorists Arrested in Germany," Knight Ridder Washington Bureau, January 24, 2005.

22. BFV, 2003.

23. Ibid. Although the latest assessment by the German foreign intelligence service noted that more than 90 percent of the Islamic extremists in Germany are Turkish, as the Germans themselves have noted, this is slightly misleading. Almost all of these Turks belong to the IGMG, a group that does not employ violence and that focuses almost entirely on Turkey itself.

24. Peter-Michael Haeberer (Berlin police chief), interview by author, January 2005.

25. Leiken, *Bearers of Global Jihad?*

26. German police officers, interviews by author, January 2005.

27. Peter Bergen, testimony before the House Committee on International Relations, "Islamic Extremism in Europe," April 27, 2005 (quoting Gilles Kepel, "The War for Muslim Minds," pp. 286–287).

28. Anonymous, *Imperial Hubris: Why the West Is Losing the War on Terror* (London: Brassey's, 2004), p. 145. "Anonymous" argues, however, that the expanded target list and the attack in Madrid were meant largely as warning shots for other Western European governments. He maintains that the last thing that bin Laden wants is for other European governments to join the war against al-Qaeda, and that therefore al-Qaeda will continue to limit its actual attacks against European targets. In fact, bin Laden did offer Europe a truce in April 2004, on the condition that it ceases support for the United States. Christopher M. Blanchard, "Al-Qaeda: Statements and Evolving Ideology," Congressional Research Service, February 4, 2005.

29. Bruce Hoffman (terrorism expert), in discussion with author, November 2004. As to the reasons bin Laden has expanded the acceptable target list, Hoffman believes that it is at least partly out of opportunism. Al-Qaeda would still prefer to attack the United States and U.S. interests, but if they aren't able to do so, they are now willing to attack non-U.S. targets as well. For example, the group responsible for the attack on the British consulate and a British bank in Istanbul was initially planning to attack a U.S. target. When this proved too difficult, they made the decision to attack a British target instead.

30. Stevenson, "Counter-terrorism."

31. Anonymous, *Through Our Enemies' Eyes* (London: Brassey's, 2003), p. 170.

32. 9-11 Commission, *Final Report*, p. 59.

33. 9-11 Commission, *Final Report*, p. 166.

34. 9-11 Commission, *Final Report*, p. 366.

35. Lorenzo Vidino (in testimony before the House International Relations Committee), April 27, 2005.

36. See Bergen, testimony before the House Committee on International Relations. Bergen also discusses why the perceived threat to the United States from graduates of Pakistani madrasas is overblown. Bergen notes that these graduates can do "little more than read the Koran and so do not have the linguistic or technical skills to make them a serious threat."

37. Sebastian Rotella, "6 Convicted in Paris in U.S. Embassy Plot," *Los Angeles Times*, March 16, 2005.

38. Tania Branigan and Suzanne Goldenberg, "Terror Plot Suspects Face Charges," *Guardian* (London), August 18, 2004.

39. "FBI: NJ al-Qaeda Spy Posed As Student," Associated Press, October 14, 2004.

40. Craig Whitlock, "In Europe, New Force for Recruiting Radicals," *Washington Post*, February 18, 2005.

41. State Department Country Report on Terrorism 2004. Available online (www.state. gov/s/ct/rls/c14813.htm).

42. Shaun Waterman, "Eurojihadis: A New Generation of Terror," United Press International, June 2, 2005. Available online (www.upi.com/view.cfm?StoryID=20050601-072835-2550r).

43. The second- and third-generation Muslims in Europe who have been radicalized—like Muhammad Bouyeri—are considered a particularly serious threat to the continental United States. For a more comprehensive look at this issue, see Leiken, "Europe's Mujahideen."

44. Cofer Black (in prepared statement before the Senate Foreign Relations Committee's Subcommittee on European Affairs), March 31, 2004.

45. Daniel Keohane (Senior Research Fellow, Center for European Reform), interview by author, January 2005. The five European countries with the most well-developed intelligence and law enforcement capabilities are Britain, France, Germany, Italy, and Spain.

46. "Europe's Terror Efforts under Scrutiny," *Deutsche Welle*, March 8, 2005. Available online (www.dw-world.de/dw/article/0,1564,1511790,00.html).

47. Author interview with senior EU official, January 2005.

48. Michael Isikoff and Mark Hosenball, "Terror Watch: On the Loose," *Newsweek,* March 16, 2005.

49. Jady Petovic, "Dutch Prosecutors to Appeal after Terrorism Trial Ends in Acquittal," Radio Netherlands, April 6, 2005. Available online (www2.rnw.nl/rnw/en/currentaffairs/region/netherlands/10786475?view=standard).

50. Sebastian Rotella, "Extremist Threats Put Netherlands in Turmoil," *Los Angeles Times,* November 22, 2004.

51. Petovic, "Dutch Prosecutors to Appeal."

52. "Dutch Government Passes New Terror Bill," Associated Press, March 4, 2005. Available online (www.kansascity.com/mld/kansascity/news/world/11055830.htm).

53. Magnus Randstorp with Jeffrey Cozzens, "European Terror Challenge," BBC News, March 24, 2004. Available online (http://newswww.bbc.net.uk/1/hi/world/europe/3563713.stm).

54. Mark Trevelyan, "Antiterror Change Urged in Europe," Reuters, November 5, 2004.

55. Craig Whitlock, "A Radical Who Remained Just out of Reach: Suspect in Madrid Attacks Moved Freely in Europe," *Washington Post*, November 14, 2004.

56. Ibid.

57. Rotella, "Extremist Threats Put Netherlands in Turmoil."

58. Daniel McGrory, "Raids Yield Clues to Europe-Wide Terrorist Network," *Times* (London), January 25, 2003.

59. Isikoff and Hosenball, "Terror Watch."

60. German police officials, interview by author, January 2005.

61. Anonymous, "Imperial Hubris," p. 99.

62. Leiken, "Europe's Mujahideen."

63. Ibid.

64. Ibid.

65. German police officers, interview by author. Right-wing politicians did not want to discuss this issue because they did not want to acknowledge that many of these foreigners were in Germany to stay. Such officials had always counted on the fact that the guest workers would return to their home eventually. Politicians on the left thought that it was unfair to force people to integrate into German society, and so preferred to leave the issue alone.

66. Klaus-Dieter Borchardt, "Structure of the European Union: The 'Three Pillars,'" in *About EU Law: The ABC of Community Law* (Belgium: European Commission, Directorate-General for Education and Culture, 2000). Available online (http://europa.eu.int/eur-lex/en/about/abc/abc_12.html).

67. European Commission, "European Arrest Warrant Replaces Extradition between EU Member States," updated May 2005. Available online (http://europa.eu.int/comm/justice_home/fsj/criminal/extradition/fsj_criminal_extradition_en.htm).

68. Ibid.

69. Author interview with senior EU official, January 2005.

70. Author interviews with European officials, January 2005.

71. "Commission Evaluation Report: The European Arrest Warrant Has Broadly Achieved Its Objectives," Europa Rapid Press Release, Memo/05/58, February 23, 2005. By February 2005, EAWs had been issued 2,603 times, 653 individuals had been arrested, and 104 had been deported.

72. "Brussels to Deport Madrid Train Bombs Suspect," Agence France Presse, March 23, 2005. Spanish authorities believe that Belhadj may be "Abou Doujanah," the European al-Qaeda spokesman who appeared on a video claiming responsibility for the Madrid attacks.

73. "Commission Evaluation Report."

74. Author interviews with European officials, January 2005.

75. Author interview with senior EU official, January 2005.

76. Author interviews with European officials, January 2005.

77. "Europe's Anti-Terror Czar Reports to Work," *Deutsche Welle*, December 31, 2004. Available online (www.dw-world.de/dw/article/0,1564,1157109,00.html).

78. Author interview with senior EU official, January 2005. In fact, the various EU members have not agreed on what De Vries's role should even be, which has certainly affected his ability to forge a coherent EU counterterrorism strategy. While some member states view his role as that of in-house expert, others see him as a senior official who represents the EU's voice on counterterrorism on the national stage.

From Reaction to Prevention

SHORTLY AFTER THE SEPTEMBER 11 ATTACKS, LEADERS at the Justice Department and FBI determined that prosecutors and law enforcement had to play a different counterterrorism role than they had in the past; this role had to be preventive in nature. Successfully investigating and prosecuting individuals after a terrorist attack—tasks at which the FBI and the Justice Department had historically performed very well—was no longer considered sufficient. On November 8, 2001, Attorney General John Ashcroft outlined his plan to reshape the department. In announcing the changes, Ashcroft stated, "[T]he attacks of September 11th have redefined the mission of the Department of Justice. Defending our nation and defending the citizens of America against terrorist attacks is now our first and overriding priority." FBI Director Robert Mueller echoed Ashcroft's comments, noting that the FBI could not be satisfied with merely reacting to attacks "with excellence" and bringing perpetrators to justice; it now had to focus on preventing them.[1]

To achieve this transformation, the Justice Department and FBI initiated numerous changes. The most noteworthy of these changes were increased prioritization of counterterrorism, more aggressive law enforcement, centralization of counterterrorism efforts, and improved information sharing between intelligence and law enforcement. In many cases, these changes would not have been possible without significant changes in the law.

A similar paradigm shift after September 11 took place in Britain and Germany, though with considerably less fanfare. British and German prosecutors and law enforcement agencies also now regarded their role in counterterrorism as largely preventive, rather than reactive. British and German law enforcement agencies made a number of significant changes in their effort to achieve this shift. Perhaps somewhat surprisingly, the changes made by the British and German law enforcement agencies have in many cases mirrored those made by the United States. They have adopted an increasingly aggressive law enforcement approach, increased the prioritization of counterterrorism, centralized their counterterrorism efforts, improved information sharing between intelligence and law enforcement agencies, and made a variety of legal changes to increase governmental ability to investigate and prosecute suspected terrorists.

Rationale for Change in Strategy

The rationale for this strategic change from reactive to preventive was similar in all three countries. The transformation was driven largely by the scale of the September 11 attacks, and by the recognition of the potential lethality of future terrorist attacks.[2] As former U.S. Justice Department assistant attorney general Viet Dinh put it, "By the time we wait to investigate, prosecute, and then incarcerate the persons, the damage is already done ... the consequence is too great, and we cannot risk that damage to the American people."[3]

The British recognized that despite their vast experience with terrorism prior to September 11, al-Qaeda terrorism represented a new and different threat—and therefore required a different response. Most of the pre-September 11 terrorist attacks in Britain were not intended to cause mass casualties. The Irish Republican Army (IRA), for example, was often focused on inflicting economic, rather than humanitarian, damage. It quickly became clear to the British that al-Qaeda, by contrast, intentionally targets the population at large.[4]

British concerns about the catastrophic potential of an al-Qaeda attack increased with post–September 11 investigative discoveries. For example, the British discovered a chemical weapons warfare protection suit during a January 2003 raid at the Finsbury Park mosque. Alarm about the discovery increased after an Algerian journalist reported that he had overheard conversations at the mosque about the possible use of chemical weapons. The journalist said that in 1999 or 2000 there were discussions at the mosque about "chemical, biological, and even a possible attack with a dirty bomb."[5] This, among other factors, is presumably what prompted Eliza Manningham-Buller, then chief of Britain's domestic intelligence service, to say in June 2003 that it was "only a matter of time" before terrorists attacked a Western country using crude chemical, biological, or nuclear weapons.[6] If September 11 was not in itself sufficient to convince the British that they needed to adopt a more aggressive and preemptive counterterrorism strategy, subsequent investigative discoveries certainly were.

German officials may differ with the United States about whether al-Qaeda and other international terrorist groups pose a strategic or a tactical threat, and whether we are currently in a "war" with terrorists. They do, however, have similar concerns about the threat of a catastrophic terrorist attack. Like Britain, Germany and many other European countries have a long history of dealing with terrorist groups. For example, in the 1970s and 1980s, the Germans fought a long battle against left-wing terrorist organizations such as the Baader-Meinhof Gang and the Red Army Faction.[7] And the Germans also recognize that Islamic terrorist groups represent a new type of terrorist threat, and that the possibility of a devastating and large-scale terrorist attack is a realistic one. The German government's concern about the possibility of a terrorist attack involving weapons of mass destruction (WMD) is evident in its decision to purchase enough vaccine to inoculate its entire population against certain types of viruses.[8] As in the United States and Britain, the fear of this type of attack has been a driving force behind the strategic shift in German law enforcement from reactive to preventive.

Prioritization of Counterterrorism

Adopting a more preventive posture has required some dramatic changes in the law enforcement agencies of the United States, Germany, and Britain. In all three countries counterterrorism has become a top concern, representing a significant change in priority. In the United States, the Justice Department and the FBI made counterterrorism their top priority almost immediately following the September 11 attacks; that shift became official on May 29, 2002, when the FBI issued a list of its top ten priorities and counterterrorism topped the register. Under this new orientation, every terrorism lead was to be addressed, even if it meant that the FBI had to transfer resources from other areas. The FBI also assigned more than a thousand additional agents to work on counterterrorism matters, and hired hundreds of new analysts and translators.[9] While national security was officially an FBI "Tier One" priority before September 11, in practice individual field offices often focused on local priorities such as drugs, gangs, and white-collar crime—and less on national priorities.[10] Director Mueller explained that the old system allowed supervisors a "great deal of flexibility" and that the new system more tightly controlled the deployment of personnel and resources.[11]

Attorney General Ashcroft also took steps to ensure that all of the U.S. Attorney's offices were adequately focused on terrorism. The Justice Department created an Anti-Terrorism Task Force at each of the ninety-three U.S. Attorney's offices, which were designed to integrate and coordinate antiterrorism field activities. (Before September 11, the New York office handled almost all high-profile terrorism prosecutions.[12]) In October 2002, the attorney general instructed every U.S. Attorney to develop a plan for monitoring terrorism and intelligence investigations, and to ensure that criminal charges were appropriately considered. Attorneys were also ordered to ensure that terrorist threat information was adequately shared with other agencies. Each U.S. Attorney's office was also ordered to designate a Chief Information Officer responsible for centralizing the information sharing process.[13] In response to Ashcroft's instructions, the U.S. Attorney's offices reviewed almost 4,500 intelligence files to determine whether criminal charges could be brought in any of these cases. Some information from this review was ultimately used in other cases.[14]

British and German law enforcement agencies made similar shifts in prioritization. The BKA (Bundeskriminalamt), the German federal law enforcement agency, made counterterrorism its top priority, followed by coordination of intelligence cooperation. To accommodate for this shift, the BKA transferred 20 percent of its investigative resources away from organized crime, its top priority in the 1990s, and reassigned them to counterterrorism matters.[15] In addition, the LKAs (Landeskriminalamt), the state law enforcement agencies, have refocused to prioritize counterterrorism. Some have shifted investigative resources from organized crime to counterterrorism, while others, such as the Berlin LKA, shifted resources from investigating immigration violations.[16] The overall budget for German law enforcement and intelligence increased by $580 million in fiscal years 2002 and 2003, with a significant percentage of this increase targeted for counterterrorism.[17] The German government also beefed up its counterterrorism prosecutorial resources by adding two new divisions to the federal prosecutor's office, which in Germany only has responsibility for prosecuting national security crimes, such as terrorism and espionage.[18]

In Britain, the Home Secretary took several steps to ensure that the police forces could adequately focus on combating terrorism. In 2004, the British government gave the Special Branches 15 million additional pounds, which the Home Secretary stated would "significantly increase their surveillance and intelligence gathering capabilities to prevent attacks against the UK."[19] The Home Secretary also created regional intelligence cells for the Special Branches, devoting three million pounds toward this effort. The Counterterrorism Branch of the Metropolitan Police received an additional twelve million pounds. The Home Secretary also updated the guidelines for the Police

Special Branches—last issued in 1994—making it clear that counterterrorism was now their top priority.[20]

Aggressive Law Enforcement

In the United States, Germany, and Britain, the "preventive strategy" has revolved around an increasingly aggressive law enforcement approach, evident in the dramatically increased number of counterterrorism arrests and raids by law enforcement agencies since September 11. As part of the preventive strategy, law enforcement agencies also take action in counterterrorism cases far earlier than they would have in the past, and they have redoubled their efforts to utilize all available legal tools to target suspected terrorists. As with the reprioritization of counterterrorism, the Justice Department and the FBI shifted to this newly aggressive approach almost immediately after September 11. Working with the Immigration and Naturalization Service, the FBI arrested almost 800 individuals for immigration violations during their investigation of the September 11 attacks. In these cases, the hearings were closed and the government sought a denial of bond until they could resolve that the prosecuted individual had no connection to terrorist activity. Ashcroft stated that this strategy was part of the Justice Department's effort to determine the perpetrators of the attacks, and also to prevent additional attacks. He expressed his determination to take every conceivable constitutional action in this regard.[21]

The Justice Department has maintained this aggressive posture in the years since September 11, arresting and charging numerous individuals for terrorism-related crimes across the United States. Those arrested in these cases have been charged with involvement in a wide variety of terrorist organizations, including al-Qaeda, Lashkar-e-Taiba, Hizballah, and others. Several examples are worth noting:

- Eleven men in Virginia were indicted for violating the Neutrality Act by training at the Lashkar-e-Taiba camps in Pakistan;

- Six individuals in Buffalo who trained at al-Qaeda camps in Afghanistan were charged with providing support to the organization;

- Cell members in North Carolina were charged with smuggling cigarettes to help fund Hizballah;

- "Shoe bomber" Richard Reid was arrested and convicted;

- Seven individuals in Portland were indicted for supporting al-Qaeda and the Taliban; and

- Eight individuals in Tampa were charged for their alleged support to the Palestinian Islamic Jihad.

By September 2003, the Justice Department had arrested and charged more than 260 individuals as a result of its newly aggressive counterterrorism investigations.[22] A key element of the United States' aggressive law enforcement strategy has been prosecuting suspected terrorists for nonterrorism-related offenses. In announcing this approach, Attorney General Ashcroft said that the Justice Department would prosecute a suspected terrorist for even "spitting on the sidewalk," noting, "It is difficult for a person in jail or under detention to murder innocent people or to aid or abet in terrorism." Ashcroft said that this approach was modeled on Attorney General Robert Kennedy's 1960s strategy to target the mafia.[23] As Viet Dinh, then assistant attorney general, explained, "If we suspect you of terrorism, you better be squeaky clean...we will arrest you, no matter how minor the violation, so that you are removed from the street and from the people you wish to harm."[24] A top Justice Department official testified that the agency also used immigration tools to target suspected terrorists, using these powers to deport suspected terrorists in situations where prosecutors either couldn't prove the case or could not expose sensitive intelligence information.[25]

While the U.S. shift has received the most publicity, the British have also mounted an increasingly aggressive law enforcement approach to combat terrorism. British aggressiveness is evident in government statistics. From September 11 to the end of 2004, the British arrested 701 people under the Terrorism Act 2000 powers. Of these, 119 were ultimately charged under the Terrorism Act; 45 of these suspects were also charged with other offenses. Moreover, 135 of those arrested under the Terrorism Act powers were charged only with nonterrorism-related offenses, such as murder and causing grievous bodily harm.[26] The dramatic increase in the number of people stopped and searched by the authorities under the counterterrorism powers of Section 44 of the 2001 act provide an even more dramatic illustration of the shift. Between 2000 and 2001, approximately 1,000 people and 2,300 vehicles were stopped and searched under Section 44. By contrast, from 2003 to 2004, British police used Section 44 powers to stop and search over 15,000 people and 4,000 vehicles. The 2000 and 2001 counterterrorism legislation will be discussed at greater length later in this study.

The British have also conducted a number of high profile counterterrorism raids and arrests, including the well-publicized January 2003 raid of the Finsbury Park Mosque in London. A group of 150 police officers wearing body armor participated in the raid, in which they used a battering ram to break down the front door of the mosque at two o'clock in the morning. In the end, seven people were arrested under the Terrorism Act 2000. Abu Hamza, the imam of the mosque, who is also a notoriously vocal Islamist, was not detained in this raid, but was later arrested.[27] In April 2004, the British police conducted an even larger-scale operation, with simultaneous raids throughout Britain, involving more than 400 officers. Ten people were arrested on the "suspicion of being concerned in the commission, preparation or instigation of acts of terrorism." A month earlier, five men were arrested and charged after British investigators seized a half ton of ammonium nitrate, the same type of fertilizer that was used in the Oklahoma City and 2002 Bali bombings.[28] One of the other raids that has received extensive publicity took place in October 2004, when the British arrested eight terrorist suspects, charging them with planning an attack using "radioactive materials, toxic gases, chemicals, and/or explosives." One of these eight individuals, Dhiren Barot, was accused by the British of having "reconnaissance plans" of buildings in the New York area and Washington, D.C., including the Prudential Building in Newark, the New York Stock Exchange, and the International Monetary Fund headquarters in Washington.[29]

This more aggressive law enforcement approach has, on at least one occasion, had deadly consequences for the British police. Police raided a Manchester house in early 2003 as part of a counterterrorism investigation in search of a North African suspect. One of the individuals in the house was able to break free and grab a knife, with which he stabbed five of the police officers—one of whom died from his wounds. Three people were arrested in the operation.[30]

The British have even taken action against some of the most visible imams, many of whom had been living in Britain and preaching freely for many years. These included Omar Mahmoud Abu Omar, a.k.a. Abu Qatada, a Palestinian with Jordanian citizenship who moved to Britain from Jordan in 1993 and successfully applied for political asylum. Qatada claimed he was trying to escape religious persecution in Jordan, although the Jordanians have accused him of being a "roving ambassador" for Osama bin Laden in Europe. Qatada was arrested in October 2002 under the indefinite detention powers of the 2001 act.[31] The former Home Secretary in Britain, David Blunkett, who made the detention decision, referred to Qatada as an "inspiration for terrorists."[32] Qatada appealed his detention but lost when the Special Immigration Appeals Commission found him to be a "truly dangerous individual," and that he was a key figure in al-Qaeda's terrorist activities in the United Kingdom.[33]

The British moved more slowly against Abu Hamza, an Egyptian-born cleric who had been living in Britain for over twenty years. Abu Hamza had been the subject of British government counterterrorism focus well prior to September 11, but even by December 2002, the British had not taken action against him. Abu Hamza was a British citizen, and thus not subject to the indefinite detention powers of the 2001 Act, which only applied to non-British citizens. In the view of the British authorities, Abu Hamza, like many other Islamic extremists, was careful to stay within the bounds of the law even while preaching his extremist message. For example, while he held an anniversary celebration for the September 11 attacks, he was presumably quite aware that he was not committing any crime by doing so. But in early 2003, the British sprang into action. Hamza was banned from preaching at the mosque, and in April 2003, the Home Office took away his citizenship, paving the way for deportation proceedings.[34]

According to the British government, the United Kingdom's newly aggressive approach has been effective in making Britain less of a sanctuary for terrorist groups. In a 2004 report, the Home Office noted, "There is intelligence to suggest that the detentions, combined with a range of other measures, have changed the environment for UK based international terrorists and that their perception of the UK has also changed as they now view it as a far more hostile place in which to operate."[35] In fact, in October 2004 the radical group al-Muhajiroun announced that it was dissolving. Long the subject of British police attention, al-Muhajiroun had openly supported the September 11 attacks and lauded the hijackers in posters as "the magnificent 19." The group's leader, Sheikh Omar Bakri Muhammad, had also warned Britain that it would be targeted by al-Qaeda if it participated in the U.S.-led war in Iraq.[36] While it is difficult to gauge whether the dissolution of al-Muhajiroun represented a true shift in the group's intentions, or whether their dissolution was the result of increased law enforcement, their formal disbanding may be another sign that Britain is becoming less of a hospitable home for extremists.

The newly aggressive posture against terrorism represents a quite radical change for the British. Prior to September 11, the United Kingdom was regarded as something of a sanctuary for terrorist suspects. In fact, London was often referred to by the French as "Londonistan" for its tolerance of Islamic militants.[37] Some believed that Britain and the Islamic extremists living there had reached a tacit understanding to coexist. As one expert stated, "The Islamists use Britain as a propaganda base but wouldn't do anything to a country that harbors them and gives them freedom of speech."[38] A former British Special Branch officer went even further, stating that there was actually a more explicit agreement between the government and the jihadists: "There was a deal with these guys. We told them if you don't cause us any problems, then we won't bother you."[39] British security officials have historically defended their tolerant approach toward extremists on two grounds. First, they said the powers of law enforcement were limited, because the extremists were not breaking any laws. Second, they argued that allowing the extremists to speak freely made it far easier for security services to monitor extremists' actions.[40]

While fear of a catastrophic attack has certainly mobilized British security services to act more aggressively, this shift in approach has also been sparked by the recognition among Britons that they have a serious terrorist problem within their own borders—and that it comes from a small number of British Muslims. As will be discussed later at greater length, even after September 11 the British believed that the threat to their country was largely external, coming mostly from individuals connected to North African terrorist groups. More recently, they have come to understand that at least a few British Muslims have also been drawn into extremism. Perhaps an even more disturbing trend is that cells in Britain, which in the past might have limited themselves to providing logistical support to terrorist operatives, are now becoming operatives themselves. According to law enforcement officials, reports of threats, over the past year in particular, have made clear to them that the danger to British interests from individuals already within the United Kingdom is a serious one.[41] In one intercepted conversation, for example, a senior militant described London as a "nerve center."[42]

Germany adopted a far more aggressive posture against Islamic terrorist threats immediately after the September 11 attacks, when it became known that some of the hijackers had lived and trained in Hamburg for years. In the wake of the attacks, the German government conducted more than 200 counterterrorism raids.[43] It wasn't immediately clear whether these raids represented just a temporary shift in German security efforts, but German law enforcement agencies have conducted numerous additional counterterrorism raids and arrests in the ensuing years. In January 2005, for example, German authorities arrested two suspected al-Qaeda members, charging them with belonging to a foreign terrorist organization. German authorities believe that these suspects were planning suicide bombings in Iraq, and perhaps even more disturbingly, alleged that the two also tried to purchase a small amount of enriched uranium.[44] These arrests followed a series of large-scale raids in early January in which 700 police officers in 6 German cities arrested 22 suspected terrorists. The German authorities seized items including forged documents and extremist literature. The chief state prosecutor has stated that some of those arrested had ties to Ansar al-Islam.[45] Three other suspected Ansar al-Islam members were arrested in December 2004, for planning to assassinate interim Iraqi Prime Minister Iyad Allawi during his trip to Germany.[46] Germany has also performed raids on over seventy mosques.[47] In addition to the raids and arrests, Germany has many other subjects under active investigation. The federal law enforcement agency has between 250 and 300 suspected international terrorists under surveillance, and the justice ministry is in the preliminary stages of proceedings against 170 suspected Islamic terrorists.[48]

The newly aggressive German stance is also evident in a changed approach to dealing with radical Islamist organizations. Since September 11, Germany has banned three organizations: Hizb-ut-Tahrir, Kalifatstaat (along with nineteen connected organizations), and the al-Aqsa Foundation.[49] The goal of Hizb-ut-Tahrir, or "Party of Liberation," is to reestablish the Islamic caliphate under one ruler. In banning Hizb-ut-Tahrir, German Interior Minister Otto Schily stated that the group was "spreading violent propaganda and anti-Jewish agitation." Hizb-ut-Tahrir has challenged the ban in court, arguing that it does not approve of al-Qaeda or its violent methods and that it is interested only in reuniting the Islamic world, not forcibly converting European countries. Germany has also attempted to expel several of the group's members, who have fought their expulsion by applying for political asylum.[50]

The Kalifatstaat is a Turkish Islamic group whose goal is first to replace the Turkish government with an Islamic one, and then to reestablish the

Islamic caliphate. The Kalifatstaat had been under observation by the German intelligence services since 1984, but no action had been taken against it until it was banned by the German government in December 2001.[51] The leader of the group, Metin Caplan, was sentenced to prison in 2004 and then extradited to Turkey in 2004.[52]

The al-Aqsa Foundation was established in 1991 in Aachen, Germany, as a "registered society" whose purpose was to raise funds for Palestinian causes. In justification for shutting it down, the German government accused the group of being a fundraising front for Hamas.[53] German officials also suspected that the group was supporting the families of suicide bombers.[54] Al-Aqsa unsuccessfully challenged the government's ban in court; as of this writing, the German government is in the process of deporting the group's founder.[55]

For Germany, as with Britain, the newly aggressive approach is a dramatic change from its pre–September 11 efforts. Germany's counterterrorism efforts prior to September 11 were ineffective and unfocused, and its law enforcement and intelligence agencies were hindered by a variety of legal obstacles. In fact, Germany was heavily criticized immediately following September 11 for its lackadaisical security efforts after the public revelations about the "Hamburg cell." German security services were portrayed as inept when, for example, it was revealed that before September 11 the foreign intelligence service was apparently not even officially tasked with investigating Islamic extremist activity.[56] This characterization of German counterterrorism has been difficult for the country to shake, and Germany is still often publicly portrayed as soft on terrorism.

Another similarity between U.S., German, and British counterterrorism approaches is that both the Germans and the British have taken a page from the American "spit on the sidewalk" approach to fighting terrorism. Like the United States, both European nations have made use of all available legal tools, including immigration powers and nonterrorism criminal statutes, to target suspected terrorists. The British have found it often very difficult to prove terrorism-related charges, and so end up charging suspected terrorists with minor offenses—at least from a sentencing standpoint—such as forging of documents or smuggling.[57] Of those detained under the Terrorism Act 2000, 230 were accused of nonterrorism-related offenses, including credit card fraud and immigration violations.[58] In Leicester, Britain, for example, a group of suspected terrorists was charged and eventually convicted for credit card fraud.[59] Of the 600 or so individuals arrested under the Terrorism Act 2000, the British have initiated immigration proceedings against approximately 50.[60]

Germany has also discovered that bringing nonterrorism-related charges against terrorist suspects is often effective, particularly in light of the significant overlap officials have discovered between terrorism and criminal activity. Germany has found, for example, that terrorist cells in the country have been involved in fraud, forgery, and drug trafficking.[61] The Germans have also made wide use of immigration laws to neutralize suspected terrorists. The use of immigration powers as a tool to target suspected terrorists seemed likely to broaden following the passage of legislation permitting the government to expel non-German nationals who pose a threat to national security.[62] In fact, the government is already putting together a list of foreign Islamists targeted for expulsion from Germany. The list is expected to include hundreds of individuals. In March 2005, the German government began enforcing the new law, deporting an imam to Turkey for threatening public safety. The imam, who had praised suicide bombers in Israel and Iraq as "martyrs," was unsuccessful in his efforts to challenge the deportation in Germany's administrative courts.[63] In addition, to make it more difficult for Islamists to become German citizens, the state immigration and citizenship departments have asked their state intelligence counterparts for information on foreigners applying for citizenship.[64]

Centralization

Another similarity in counterterrorism approaches is that the United States, Germany, and (to a lesser extent) Britain each identified decentralization of law enforcement agencies as a hindrance to counterterrorism effectiveness before September 11. All countries have taken steps since then centralize their counterterrorism efforts.

Before September 11, FBI counterterrorism investigations were managed by individual field offices in the United States. The FBI had a system, referred to as the "office of origin," under which a single office was in charge of an entire investigation. For example, the New York field office was the office of origin for all bin Laden cases. According to the 9-11 Commission, the result was that other field offices (those that were not the office of origin) were "reluctant to spend much energy on matters over which they had no control and for which they received no credit." Individual field offices often focused instead on issues of local concern, such as drugs, gangs, and white-collar crime, and less on national priorities like counterterrorism.[65] Director Mueller instituted policies giving FBI headquarters control for directing and coordinating counterterrorism investigations. The primary purpose behind the change was to ensure a more consistent counterterrorism strategy across the agency, and to improve coordination and information sharing.[66]

The concept of decentralization was integrated into Germany's national security apparatus in the wake of World War II, in an effort to prevent a centralized authority from assuming too much power or possessing too much information. While Germany had a federal law enforcement agency (BKA), policing was generally considered a state matter, and authority for law enforcement resided primarily with the sixteen states (Lander). The BKA had limited control over the state level agencies.[67]

In an effort to overcome these barriers and to centralize law enforcement (and intelligence) efforts, German Interior Minister Otto Schily established in December 2004 an intelligence center in Berlin at which all of the federal and state intelligence and law enforcement agencies have a presence.[68] He described the center as a "qualitative leap" forward in Germany's counterterrorism efforts.[69] Concerned that Germany's federal intelligence and law enforcement agencies were scattered throughout the country, he attempted to move the headquarters of all the various agencies to Berlin.[70]

It should be noted that while Schily has taken major steps to centralize Germany's law enforcement and intelligence efforts, he has not been entirely successful in this regard. He has, for example, unsuccessfully sought more "preventive powers" for the BKA, which would put it on equal footing with the state law enforcement agencies. With these powers, the federal law enforcement agency could take on more of a national and central role in Germany's counterterrorism efforts, instead of having to leave primacy in these investigations to the states—an administrative feature that leaves the country much more vulnerable to coordination and information sharing problems, in the view of senior German federal law enforcement officials.[71] Schily's effort to move all of the federal intelligence and law enforcement agencies was also not entirely successful. For example, while the foreign intelligence service moved its headquarters operations to Berlin in the fall of 2003, only a third of BKA's organizational structure was ultimately moved, and the domestic intelligence service headquarters remained in Cologne.[72] Schily's limited success in this arena is not surprising; there is still a great deal of resistance in Germany, in light of its history, to any attempts to centralize power, particularly at the federal level.

U.S. attempts to centralize counterterrorism efforts in Washington have also been far from a complete success. As in Germany, the historically troubled relationship between federal, state, and local counterterrorism officials remains a particularly difficult obstacle to overcome. The FBI and the New York Police Department (NYPD), for example, have had a number of public feuds since September 11 about their respective counterterrorism roles. In fact, the NYPD made the decision after the attacks to create its own counterterrorism office, believing that it could not—and should not—rely solely on the federal government to protect the city from a terrorist attack.[73]

Britain has likewise taken steps to centralize its counterterrorism efforts, though this is less of an issue for the British than for the United States or Germany, which are both federal systems with powerful, independent states in which authority is far more widely dispersed. The British created the position of "national coordinator" for counterterrorism investigations, appointing the deputy assistant commissioner of the Metropolitan Police to this position. The national coordinator was given responsibility for coordinating investigations run by law enforcement agencies throughout the country, though only in situations where the local chief constable approved.[74] The British also created the position of security and intelligence coordinator and permanent secretary in the Cabinet Office. This person is responsible for overseeing the United Kingdom's domestic counterterrorism efforts, and serves as an adviser to the prime minister on these matters.[75]

Information Sharing between Intelligence and Law Enforcement

While all of the changes described above have certainly helped U.S., British, and German law enforcement assume a more preventive role in counterterrorism, perhaps the most vital change has been improved information sharing and closer coordination between the domestic intelligence services and law enforcement agencies. Law enforcement agencies are obviously only able to take preemptive action when they have actionable intelligence. In the past, there were many cases in which intelligence services did not share information with law enforcement. This has changed, to some extent, in all three countries.

One reason that improved information sharing leads to a more preventive law enforcement approach is that, by its nature, law enforcement calculation of when to take action is different from that of the intelligence services. If they believe there is a serious danger or an imminent crime, law enforcement officials will want to take action. Intelligence services—in the view of at least one senior law enforcement official—are more inclined to postpone action in an effort to gather as much intelligence as possible.[76] Whether or not this assessment is accurate, it is certainly the case that prior to September 11, intelligence services controlled the decisions of law-enforcement action because they were often the only ones to know about a particular case or threat. Because this is no longer true, law enforcement agencies now play a far more important role in the decisionmaking process.

The United States government has highlighted improved information sharing between intelligence and law enforcement as one of the most important post–September 11 developments. According to the Justice Department, as a result of these changes, now a "complete mosaic of information can be compiled," allowing those investigating terrorism to better connect the dots.[77] In the United States, improved information sharing is due largely to changes in the law. As has been well documented, before September 11 there was a "wall" between FBI intelligence components and FBI criminal investigators (and Justice Department prosecutors).[78] As both a domestic intelligence and law enforcement agency, the FBI had tools for both intelligence and law enforcement matters. One of the tools at the FBI's disposal was surveillance, available under the 1978 Foreign Intelligence Surveillance Act (FISA). FISA permitted the sharing of relevant information with law enforcement, but required that the "purpose" of the surveillance be to collect foreign intelligence information. Courts later interpreted the term "purpose" to mean that the government must demonstrate that the "primary purpose" was to obtain foreign intelligence information. The underlying rationale behind this requirement was to prevent the government from circumventing the more stringent criminal warrant requirements. The Justice Department became concerned that a court might rule that a FISA surveillance was illegal because collecting foreign intelligence was not the "primary purpose." To prevent this from occurring, the Justice Department created procedures to govern information sharing between intelligence and criminal-investigative components.[79] These procedures were almost immediately, according to the 9-11 Commission, "misunderstood and misapplied." By September 11, the wall had taken on almost mythic proportions, and there was a widespread misperception that the FBI could not share any intelligence information at all—not just FISA information—with criminal investigators.[80]

The Patriot Act was the first step in dismantling the wall.[81] Section 218 of the act changed the "primary purpose" standard to allow the use of FISA as long as foreign intelligence was a "significant purpose" of the surveillance. In November 2002, the never-before-convened FISA Court of Review took the next important step in bringing down the wall. The FISA court was convened to hear an appeal by the government of an order issued by the lower FISA court. That court had approved the Justice Department's new information sharing procedures, but only with modifications that in many ways kept the wall intact. The lower court had instructed the FBI and the Criminal Division of the Justice Department to ensure that law enforcement officials did not "direct or control" the FISAs to enhance criminal prosecution, even inadvertently. On November 18, 2002, the FISA Court of Review affirmed the Justice Department's position, dismissing the lower FISA court's concerns about prosecutors directing and controlling FISAs, and noting, "So long as the government entertains a realistic option of dealing with an agent other than through criminal prosecution, it satisfies the significant purpose test."[82]

The Patriot Act also was designed to improve information flow in the reverse direction—from law enforcement to intelligence personnel. Section 203(a) of the act allows the disclosure of grand jury information to "any federal law enforcement, intelligence, protective, immigration, national defense, or national security" official, in order to assist the official in the performance of his official duties. Section 905 requires all federal law enforcement agencies to expeditiously disclose to the Director of Central Intelligence any foreign intelligence information collected in the course of a criminal investigation. The December 2004 intelligence reform act was another big step toward the increase of information flow, allowing federal prosecutors to share grand jury information with foreign governments and with states.[83]

According to the Justice Department, improved coordination between intelligence and law enforcement has yielded concrete benefits. There have been many successful prosecutions, which the Justice Department maintains would not have been possible without these legal (and accompanying cultural) changes. These include prosecution of the so-called "Portland Seven," who attempted to travel to Afghanistan in 2001 and 2002 to fight with the Taliban and al-Qaeda. In this case, law enforcement agents learned from an informant that one member of the cell, Jeffrey Battle, apparently had considered attacking Jewish schools or synagogues, and had even conducted some casing of possible targets. Due to the dismantling of the information sharing wall, it was clear that the FBI could keep prosecutors informed as to developments from the FISA surveillance of Battle. Ultimately, Battle and six other defendants were charged. Six of the defendants were convicted and sentenced to prison, while charges against the seventh were dismissed after he died in Pakistan.

The Justice Department has also pointed to a number of other cases in which improved information sharing between intelligence and law enforcement has been crucial to a successful resolution. These include the "Lackawanna Six," who will be discussed at greater length later, and the case of Latif Dumeisi, who was convicted in January 2004 of illegally acting as an Iraqi government agent. The Justice Department also contends that the Patriot Act was instrumental in the investigation and prosecution of suspected Palestinian Islamic Jihad members (including Sami al-Arian), by allowing prosecutors to see all of the evidence, including information collected under FISA, and then to bring appropriate charges.[84]

Increased information sharing and improved coordination between intelligence and law enforcement agencies in Britain and Germany have also been integral in allowing law enforcement agencies in those countries to adopt a more preventive posture. In both Germany and Britain, the intelligence services are in many cases coordinating and sharing information with law enforcement at a far earlier stage than they have in the past.[85] As a result, law enforcement agencies are able to take action earlier.

According to Peter Clarke, the head of the Anti-Terrorist Branch of the Metropolitan Police, one of the most notable features of the post–September 11 world is the close relationship that has developed between MI-5, the British domestic intelligence service, and the police. The old concept of a "firewall" between law enforcement and intelligence is now gone, in the view of Clarke, who heads an interagency committee that reviews ongoing cases.[86] As one senior Scotland Yard official stated, "The police are now involved in things that ten years ago, MI-5 would have had fits about."[87] In fact, two new units were created after September 11 inside MI-5, charged with analyzing intelligence and communicating with the police forces.[88]

As a result of the closer cooperation with law enforcement, MI-5 has increasingly begun to operate in an evidential framework. MI-5's resources for seeking legal advice, for example, have been substantially increased. According to Clarke, upcoming terrorism prosecutions will reveal the shift in the way MI-5 collects information, and demonstrate that MI-5 is increasingly collecting information that can be used in criminal proceedings.[89] While September 11 was the most important catalyst, the shift was set into motion well before the attacks. Experts believe that it can probably be traced to 1996, when MI-5 was first given responsibility for investigating serious crime.[90]

British prosecutors are also now far more integrated into the investigative process, working more closely with the police. In the past, prosecutors were typically not brought into the investigation until the very end. In fact, there was often animosity between the police and prosecutors, as the police regarded the prosecutors as overly averse to taking risks. One police official, for example, referred to the Crown Prosecution Service (CPS) as the "Criminals Protection Society." The former British attorney general acknowledged that, historically, prosecutors and police had not worked together closely. In his view, this had to change, noting that "they mustn't be divided; they must work very closely" together to prepare cases for court.[91]

In an effort to better integrate prosecutors and police, the head of the CPS initiated a pilot project that situated prosecutors full-time at police stations, allowing them to advise police at early stages of investigations. The goal was to reduce the number of cases in which prosecutors dropped or altered those charges initially brought by police. Based on the success of the pilot project, the CPS introduced this program countrywide in 2003. While the project was not specifically designed with counterterrorism in mind, closer coordination between prosecutors and police has been beneficial in the counterterrorism arena as well.[92]

Britain, like the United States, can point to specific cases where improved coordination and information sharing between intelligence and law enforcement has resulted in the successful prosecution of terrorism suspects. One such example in Britain was the prosecution of Sajid Badat, an associate of "shoe bomber" Richard Reid. Badat had been the subject of a long-running inquiry by MI-5, which suspected him of being connected to al-Qaeda. MI-5 coordinated its investigation with the police, who arrested Badat in November 2003 and charged him with various terrorism-related offenses.[93] Badat pleaded guilty to some of these charges in February 2005. The January 2003 police counterterrorism operation in

Manchester, during which three suspects were arrested, was also an "intelligence-led operation." As will be discussed later, one of the suspects in that case was also convicted of terrorism charges.[94]

The closer coordination between intelligence and law enforcement represents a dramatic shift. In the past, MI-5 would conduct information gathering and decide when to bring in the police. There would be a formal "handoff point." MI-5 would then draft an intelligence report for the police. Law enforcement agencies, in turn, would use this report as their starting point, but would still have to independently prove every fact alleged in the report, because the intelligence information was not considered "evidence."[95]

In Germany, as in the United States and Britain, the wall between intelligence and law enforcement agencies has been somewhat dismantled—though not to the degree that it has been in Britain and the United States. Law enforcement agencies are now aware of intelligence services' cases far earlier. In fact, the head of the federal law enforcement and intelligence agencies now meet once a week in Berlin, and the federal prosecutor joins them once a month. At these meetings the intelligence services, law enforcement agencies, and prosecutors all discuss how to use intelligence information in a criminal proceeding. The intelligence services are even beginning to become more accustomed to the possibility that their work product may end up in court.[96] Improving cooperation and communication between Germany's law enforcement and intelligence services has been a difficult challenge and has required both legal and structural changes. Many of the barriers between intelligence and law enforcement were integrated into Germany's national security apparatus after World War II. As with decentralization, this barrier was an effort to prevent the concentration of too much power or information in any one entity; separation between intelligence and law enforcement in Germany was considered to have the force of constitutional law.[97] Coordination and cooperation were made even more difficult because every one of Germany's sixteen states has its own intelligence and law enforcement agency.

Despite the historical rationale for separation between intelligence and law enforcement, closer relations between the two were deemed necessary after September 11 because of the increased threat posed by Islamic terrorist groups. Klaus Buss, the chairman of the German interior minister conference, said it was "absolutely necessary that we take full advantage of information retrieval," because Islamic terrorism poses a very serious danger for an "indefinite period."[98] The driving force behind the information sharing changes, as with increased centralization, has been Otto Schily, the German federal interior minister. As noted above, Schily established in December 2004 an intelligence center in Berlin. Here all federal and state intelligence and law enforcement agencies have a presence (though because of legal restrictions, law enforcement and intelligence agencies at the center still do not have access to all of the other agencies' information).[99] In the view of BKA President Jorg Ziercke, the center should help Germany improve coordination and information sharing by developing a "network of information."[100]

Another effort to improve information sharing in Germany has been the attempted establishment of a database of suspected terrorists that will be accessible to all intelligence and law enforcement agencies. Accessibility to the database will require a change in law because of the required separation between German law enforcement and intelligence entities.[101] There has been speculation that this change will only be made if a third post–September 11 legislative package is passed.

In Britain, unlike Germany and the United States, improved cooperation between intelligence services and law enforcement has not been the result of either legal or structural changes. While cooperation between intelligence and law enforcement was problematic in Britain before September 11, the problem was not caused by legal or structural barriers, but by cultural issues. Britain has made legal changes, however, that have improved information sharing throughout the government, and presumably will benefit law enforcement and intelligence agencies as well. Part three of the 2001 Antiterrorism Act allowed government agencies to share information not only in terrorism investigations but also in any criminal investigation, including investigations outside the United Kingdom.[102]

While legislative changes have been at the core of improved information sharing in Germany and the United States, there have also been a variety of nonlegislative changes in those two countries that have increased law enforcement's access to important counterterrorism information. For example, in an effort to improve information sharing between law enforcement agencies and their foreign counterparts, both Germany and the United States have dramatically increased the number of law enforcement representatives in foreign postings. After the September 11 attacks, the FBI increased the number of its overseas offices from approximately twenty-five to almost fifty.[103] These new offices were in locations of importance to the FBI's counterterrorism work, including the United Arab Emirates, Malaysia, and Morocco.[104] The BKA, likewise, had a considerable number of officers overseas before September 11, most of them focused on organized crime and other criminal cases, not counterterrorism. After the attacks, the BKA shifted the focus of many of its officers to counterterrorism, in some cases relocating officers to posts with greater importance for the counterterrorism mission, including a number of North African countries, the Arabian Peninsula, and Indonesia.[105]

Both the United States and Germany have also made use of domestic terrorism task forces to improve information sharing between various law enforcement agencies. The FBI uses the Joint Terrorism Task Force (JTTF) concept, created in 1980 in response to a series of domestic terrorist incidents.[106] Since September 11, the FBI has greatly expanded its use of JTTFs, which include the FBI as well as other federal, state, and local law enforcement agencies. As of September 11, there were thirty-five JTTFs in the United States.[107] As of June 2005, approximately a hundred were operating throughout the country.[108] Germany has also historically employed the task force concept in counterterrorism investigations, dating back to the days when it was investigating the Red Army Faction. German counterterrorism task forces can include state and local law enforcement, border police, and other federal law enforcement agencies.[109] After their connections to the September 11 attacks became clear, Germany quickly put together an investigative task force that included 600 BKA officers—the largest ever assembled in that country. Germany also has task forces in place in several states where al-Qaeda affiliate Ansar al-Islam is considered a particularly serious threat.[110]

Other Legal Changes

While the legal changes breaking down walls between intelligence gathering and law enforcement were very important—particularly in the United States and Germany—they were not the only significant legal changes made by the United States, Britain, and Germany in the wake of the September 11 attacks. All three countries have made numerous other legal changes that have increased the ability of their respective law enforcement agencies to target and prosecute suspected terrorists. In many cases, the paradigm shift for law enforcement and prosecution from reactive to preemptive would have been far more difficult—if not impossible—without these legal changes.

After the September 11 attacks, all three countries passed major counterterrorism legislative packages, and each has adopted additional legal changes since then. In the United States, most of the legal changes were included in the USA PATRIOT Act, a comprehensive legislative package passed in October 2001. Other significant changes were codified in the Intelligence Reform and Terrorism Prevention Act of 2004 (IRTPA), which was signed into law in December of that year. In Germany, two primary pieces of post–September 11 counterterrorism legislation had passed as of June 2005: the first in October 2001 and the second in January 2003. In Britain, the legislature passed a fairly comprehensive law in late 2001, pledging that it would "build on legislation in a number of areas to ensure that the government, in light of the new situation arising from the September 11 terrorist attacks on New York and Washington, have the necessary powers to counter the threat to the U.K."[111] This legislation surprised some observers, because in 2000 Britain had already passed wide-ranging and comprehensive legislation dealing with international terrorism, at least partly in response to the growing threat of Islamic terrorism.[112] Before 2000, Britain only had emergency counterterrorism powers, and those dealt solely with terrorism connected with the affairs of Northern Ireland ("Irish Terrorism"). The Terrorism Act 2000 was introduced to provide permanent U.K.-wide legislation applicable to all forms of terrorism: Irish, international, and domestic.[113] The British passed additional counterterrorism-related legislation in March 2005.

Media portrayal of laws changed after September 11 has characterized the United States as making more dramatic changes than those in other Western democracies. The reality is more nuanced. While there are areas in which the United States has enacted more far-reaching laws, in other areas the British and German laws allow their respective law enforcement agencies and prosecutors to take more intrusive action than their U.S. counterparts. It should be noted that the legal changes made in all three countries are extraordinarily complex, detailed, and lengthy—and could easily be the sole subject of a separate book. The purpose of this section is not to serve as a comprehensive guide to legal reforms, but merely to highlight some of the most important developments affecting law enforcement and counterterrorism prosecution.

Increased Power for Law Enforcement

After September 11, the United States instituted a variety of legal changes designed to increase the ability of law enforcement to investigate suspected terrorists and to prevent future terrorist attacks. One particularly important aspect of the Patriot Act in this regard, which has received surprisingly little attention, was that it updated the law to reflect changes in technology. For example, the Patriot Act clarifies that certain investigative techniques apply not only to telephone communications but also to the internet. Former Assistant Attorney General Viet Dinh described this change as "one of the most vital in the war on terrorism," because it allowed law enforcement to monitor terrorists' communications "regardless of which medium" the terrorists use.[114] The Patriot Act also authorizes judges to issue roving wiretaps, which could include any phone or computer that the suspect might use nationwide, instead of ones limited to a given judge's jurisdiction.

In addition, the Patriot Act increased the FBI's ability to obtain information from third parties in national security investigations. One such tool—which was available to the FBI prior to the passage of the Patriot Act, but was expanded by the act—is a National Security Letter (NSL). NSLs are a type of administrative subpoena available to the FBI in international terrorism and foreign counterintelligence investigations, used to obtain such items as telephone, financial, and electronic communication records. While the FBI had the statutory authority to use NSLs for many years before September 11, the Patriot Act changed the NSL statutes by dramatically loosening the standard for their use, and by simplifying and decentralizing the FBI's approval process for issuing NSLs. Before passage of the Patriot Act, the FBI could use NSLs only to obtain the records of suspected terrorists or of spies. Now, the FBI is able to use NSLs when the information sought is merely relevant to an authorized international terrorism or foreign counterintelligence investigation. Moreover, before September 11, few individuals aside from senior officials at FBI headquarters in Washington could approve the issuance of NSLs. The Patriot Act lowered this hurdle by granting FBI field office executives authority to approve NSLs.[115]

Through the Patriot Act, the Justice Department and FBI can seek— via a FISA court order—individuals' business records from third parties, including libraries.[116] This power—which has become a lightning rod in the debate surrounding the Patriot Act—is similar to that available in ordinary criminal investigations, in which grand juries can issue subpoenas to all types of businesses.

The most significant change by IRTPA in terms of law enforcement's counterterrorism powers involved amending FISA to allow the FBI to

obtain wiretaps and conduct secret searches on individual terrorist suspects who have no connection to a foreign power. Several members of
Congress had been pushing for the change, driven in part by revelations
that the FBI did not obtain a FISA wiretap on accused September 11 conspirator Zacarias Moussaoui before the attacks because FBI lawyers did
not believe there was sufficient information to connect him to a foreign
power.[117] FBI and Justice Department officials supported the change,
arguing that there is increasing danger from lone actors who may sym-
pathize with the larger causes of formal terrorist groups, even if they
have little or no connection to these groups.[118] While wiretaps and secret
searches are intelligence and not law enforcement tools, broader latitude
by the FBI to collect intelligence information should be felt among prosecutors and the law enforcement side of the FBI as well, given the fact
that the "wall" between intelligence and law enforcement is no longer in
place.[119]

In addition to the many post–September 11 legal changes in U.S.
counterterrorism law enforcement, there have been important policy
changes. After September 11, the Justice Department revised its internal investigative guidelines to allow law enforcement agents more freedom in their investigations. The old guidelines generally barred the
FBI from using the internet to access information except when it was
investigating specific cases. There was also no clear authority under
the old guidelines for FBI agents to attend events open to the general
public, unless they already had evidence of some criminal activity. The
new guidelines give the FBI the same access to public events, places,
and information that the general public has, with certain safeguards to
prevent abuse. Under the old guidelines the FBI could only visit public
events for the purpose of "detecting or preventing terrorist activity,"
and could not retain information gathered unless it related to potential
criminal or terrorist activity."[120]

Like the United States, Britain and Germany have adopted a number
of legal changes that have increased the ability of law enforcement agencies to act preemptively in the counterterrorism arena. In Britain, the most
important changes were made in the Terrorism Act 2000, which gave
law enforcement much broader powers to investigate terrorism. The act
allowed the police to make arrests without warrants in situations when
the officer had reasonable suspicion that the individual was involved in
terrorism. Police were also authorized by the act to detain suspected ter-

rorists for up to seven days without charge—although this detention had to be approved by a judge after forty-eight hours—and to search individuals whom they could legally arrest as suspected terrorists. This detention power was extended in 2003 in a criminal justice bill, allowing the police (subject to court approval) to detain terrorist suspects for fourteen days instead of seven.[121] The 2000 act also permitted police to cordon off areas for up to fourteen days during a terrorist investigation, with a maximum extension to twenty-eight days. In addition, it allowed police to obtain information from third parties—specifically, financial institutions—more easily, through the use of a "disclosure order."[122]

While these changes certainly represented a dramatic increase in British law enforcement's counterterrorism powers, by far the most controversial provision of the 2000 act was the now notorious "Section 44," which allowed the police to stop and search people and their vehicles in certain designated geographical areas.[123] The reason for the controversy is that the stop and search power does not require the police to have particular cause for suspicion within the approved areas. In other words, within a designated geographical area, the police can stop and search anyone for any reason—though the search may only be for articles "of a kind which could be used in connection with terrorism." These authorizations have been used at one point or another in almost every part of Britain; London has been continuously designated as a "Section 44" area.[124]

While the Terrorism Act 2000 was probably more significant for British law enforcement than the subsequent Anti-Terrorism, Crime, and Security Act 2001, the 2001 act did make some additional changes of note, particularly in terms of law enforcement's ability to obtain information from third parties. For example, the 2001 act increased—beyond what was mandated in the 2000 act—the amount of information police could request from financial institutions.[125] In addition, the 2001 act changed the data retention requirements for communications providers, by increasing the amount of time they were required to retain data, and by making it easier for law enforcement and intelligence agencies to obtain such information.[126] Finally, one particularly important, but unrelated, change in the 2001 legislation allowed the government to involuntarily fingerprint individuals suspected of terrorist activity.

In Germany, perhaps the most important changes in terms of counterterrorism law enforcement were made in the first of two counterterrorism legislative packages, passed in October 2001. The package removed a key loophole in German law, which prior to September 11 had significantly restricted investigation of Islamic terrorism. This loophole—the so-called "religious privilege protection"—shielding religious organizations from governmental intrusion. Islamic terrorist groups in Germany had taken advantage of this law, which effectively allowed them to operate without concern that they were being targeted by the government. The first legislative package changed the law and allowed the government to both investigate and ban religious groups.[127]

The second legislative package was designed to improve the ability of government agencies to collect information about terrorist suspects, in many cases from third parties. German intelligence services were given the authority to demand suspect information from a wide variety of institutions, including banks and other financial institutions, the post office, airlines, and telecommunication companies. These third parties were prohibited from disclosing the requests to the customers about whom intelligence was being requested. Domestic intelligence agency jurisdiction was also expanded, allowing authorities to gather information on "endeavors that are directed against the idea of international understanding, especially against the peaceful coexistence of people."[128] Given closer coordination and improved information sharing between intelligence and law enforcement, these changes should also benefit German law enforcement agencies. The second legislative package also increased the German government's ability to expel foreigners, by permitting the expulsion of non-German nationals deemed a national security risk.[129]

Other legal changes not included in the two packages have also increased German law enforcement's investigative capabilities, in particular their access to data from third parties. In October 2001, the German parliament passed a law mandating that telecommunication companies, not including internet service providers, update their systems by January 2005 to ensure that police and intelligence agencies could access communications when necessary. These proposals had apparently been under discussion for over five years, and had stalled over privacy and cost concerns, but were pushed forward after the September 11 attacks.[130] Finally, several nonlegislative changes have also improved law enforcement access to data in counterterrorism investigations. For example, the German phone companies now have set up a twenty-four-hour center that provides assistance and information to law enforcement agencies.[131]

Increased Power to Prosecute Suspected Terrorists

In the United States, both the Patriot Act and IRTPA ushered into law changes allowing the Justice Department to adopt a more preventive counterterrorism approach, by enabling the government to more easily prosecute suspected terrorists. The most significant changes appear to have been those related to "material support" of terrorism. As will be discussed at greater length below, material support prosecution has been the cornerstone of the Justice Department's more aggressive counterterrorism efforts since September 11.

Some background: Title 18, Section 2339A, of the Antiterrorism and Effective Death Penalty Act of 1996 makes it a crime to provide material support or resources that a donor knows will be used in connection with a terrorist act. Section 2339B prohibits "knowingly" providing material support or resources to organizations designated as "foreign terrorist organizations." As defined by the statute, "material support and resources" include financial assets, training, communications equipment, safe houses, and other facilities, as well as other physical assets. The Patriot Act amended the statute, adding "expert advice and assistance" to the list of prohibited types of support. The Patriot Act also clarified that "material support" did not just mean hard currency, but all forms of money. Finally, the Patriot Act increased the maximum penalty for providing material support to terrorists from ten to fifteen years.

For the Justice Department, the Patriot Act made it easier to prosecute individuals believed to be funneling money to terrorists. Before the act passed, people operating unlicensed money-transmitting businesses—which could include the informal Arab brokerage systems called *hawalas*—were allowed to plead that they had no knowledge of the state licensing requirements.[132] Section 373 of the Patriot Act made it more difficult for these types of companies to plead ignorance, by requiring that individuals involved in money-transmitting businesses know about the state licensing requirements. IRTPA added to the "material support" statute by making it a criminal offense to "knowingly receive" military-type training from a designated terrorist organization. In the past, even if someone confessed to knowingly attending an al-Qaeda training camp, that alone would not have been an illegal act. IRTPA also clarified the definition of certain aspects of the statute after the Ninth U.S. Circuit Court of Appeals found them to be unconstitutionally vague.[133]

Like the United States, Germany and Britain made a variety of legal changes to improve their ability to prosecute suspected terrorists and take on a more preventive counterterrorism role. Germany made one particularly significant change after September 11 in this regard, by closing another loophole. Before September 11, it was not illegal to plan a terrorist act intended to take place outside of Germany, or to be a member of a foreign terrorist organization. In other words, it was not illegal for an al-Qaeda member in Germany to plan a terrorist attack against the United States. In order for a crime to have taken place, Germany would have had to prove that the terrorist organization in question was actually based in Germany. In its first post–September 11 legislative package, Germany changed this law; it can now prosecute members of terrorist organizations, even if those organizations are based outside of Germany.[134]

In Britain, the Terrorism Act 2000 effected a series of far-reaching changes designed to enable the British to more easily prosecute suspected terrorists. The 2000 act revolved around the idea of "proscription," which allows the government to designate certain organizations as terrorist groups. The act then expanded the reach of prosecutors by criminalizing individuals' actions when they were associated with a proscribed organization. The authority for proscribing terrorist organizations was granted by the act to the Home Secretary, who was given broad power and wide discretion in his proscription decisions. In March 2001, the Home Secretary released the initial list of proscribed organizations, which included al-Qaeda, Egyptian Islamic Jihad, and Hamas.[135] The list of terrorist organizations is constantly kept under review, and updated when necessary by the Home Secretary, subject to parliamentary approval.[136]

The 2000 act also criminalized various proscription-related offenses. For example, the legislation barred individuals from belonging to or even professing that they were members of a proscribed organization. The burden of proof of belonging was shifted in these cases from the government to the person charged with the offense. To avoid conviction, the person charged had to demonstrate that he either was not involved with the group when it became proscribed, or that the group was not proscribed when he became a member. Ignorance of the group's proscription status was not an acceptable defense.[137] The act also prohibited action "on any level" that furthered the activities of the organization. This was broadly defined to include not only financial support, but also such actions as organizing a proscribed group's meetings, or even having one of the proscribed organization's members speak at a meeting. Also prohibited were wearing items of clothing associated with that organization or displaying an article of clothing that would reasonably lead to suspicion that you were a member in the proscribed organization.[138]

While proscription and proscription-related offenses were at the heart of the Terrorism Act 2000, the legislation gave prosecutors other powerful counterterrorism tools as well. For example, the act placed an affirmative duty on members of the public to report to the police information that might enable them to prevent a terrorist attack. The act also made it an offense to possess information that might be useful to terrorists, whether or not the person having the information intended to use it for terrorist purposes.[139] And the act shifted the burden of proof in these types of cases, requiring the person charged to demonstrate that he did not possess the information for any type of terrorist-related purpose.[140] The 2001 act subsequently expanded a person's obligation to report to authorities information that might help prevent a terrorist attack. Under the 2000 act, this duty was limited to information obtained in a work context, but the 2001 legislation made neglecting to report such information an offense in any situation. Finally, the 2000 act criminalized various other actions, including inciting terrorism overseas, engaging in terrorist training (either in Britain or overseas), and providing instruction that might be helpful to commit terrorist acts, such as in firearms or explosives.[141]

Are U.S. Changes More Far-Reaching?

The widespread perception in the United States and in Europe is that the legal changes in the United States after September 11, particularly those codified in the Patriot Act, are more dramatic than corresponding changes in other democracies. This assessment is only partly accurate, and caused by misperceptions of the Patriot Act. Many people believe inaccurately, for example, that the most controversial U.S. actions—such as the detention of enemy combatants at Guantanamo Bay—have been conducted under the aegis of the Patriot Act.

In some respects German and British law enforcement authorities are more constrained in counterterrorism investigations than are their U.S. counterparts, but there are also aspects in which the German and British legal changes have been more far-reaching than those made by the United States. Consider the law enforcement technique of "grid searching." Grid searching is a form of profiling that allows law enforcement to use sophisticated technological searches to identify individuals who match certain "criminal" profiles. Grid searching was legal in Germany before September 11, but in most German states it was permissible only in the context of "imminent danger." After September 11, some of these states made legislative changes in order to liberalize the use of this technique. For example, one state now allows police to conduct this type of search when it is "necessary for the preventive fight against crimes of considerable significance." Grid searching is now legal in several German states where it was previously prohibited.[142]

Both federal and state law enforcement agencies in Germany made use of grid searching after September 11. As one search parameter, the federal government targeted Muslim male students from certain countries between the ages of 18 and 40. This profile resulted in approximately 1,150 "hits," which were followed up by additional police investigations.[143] Although German law enforcement agencies still consider grid searching to be a potentially effective tool in combating terrorism, coordinating the differing state legislation and nonexisting federal legislation on the subject has often proved time consuming and labor intensive. Nevertheless, German security agencies are attempting to improve their grid searching capabilities, and to devise a system that will allow for better-coordinated nationwide searches.[144]

By contrast, a United States proposal to develop a comprehensive profiling capability after September 11 met with far greater backlash than did the German effort. The Defense Department created the Total Information Awareness project, which was designed to search through publicly available data to identify patterns of activity that might indicate a terrorist plot. Following considerable negative publicity, the Senate blocked funding for the program in January 2003, effectively shutting it down at the time. The German effort, though somewhat controversial, was allowed to proceed and remained a legal technique used by law enforcement agencies.[145] One reason that German law enforcement agencies were able to utilize the grid searching technique is that, in many cases, the German government has more information about its residents than does the United States. Individuals living in Germany—both citizens and foreign nationals—have to register their addresses and phone numbers with police, and must also provide a list of all housemates. Germans are also required to notify the police whenever they move.[146] And Germany can now prosecute an individual for being a member of a foreign terrorist organization, which is something that the United States still cannot do. In the United States, the government must prove that an individual took some action on behalf of a terrorist organization; membership alone is not a crime. The United States has instead frequently relied on evidence that the person provided "material support" to terrorists to achieve the same goals.

Nevertheless, there are still ways in which the German government's ability to gather information remains far more constrained than that of the United States. German law enforcement agencies are limited not only by Germany's data protection laws—which remain the strictest in Europe— but also by cultural resistance to governmental intrusion. Privacy rights are explicitly written into Germany's constitution (the "Basic Law") and the German Constitutional Court has affirmed this principle, ruling that an individual has the right of "information self-determination."

As data protection is considered an important element of individual privacy, Germany has created an entire bureaucracy whose purpose is ensuring appropriate levels of protection of personal data. The Federal Data Protection Commission, an independent federal agency, is charged with overseeing the implementation of the Federal Data Protection Act. In addition, every one of Germany's sixteen states has its own data protection laws overseen by a data protection commissioner. In late September 2001, a proposal to create a law akin to the U.S. Freedom of Information Act, which would allow Germans more access to government information, was dropped.[147]

Even where collecting data is legal, however, German law enforcement agencies often encounter significant other difficulties. For example, the German government's profiling efforts after the September 11 attacks were approved by the courts but generated privacy-related concerns and ran into serious obstacles. As part of their investigation, police sent out requests to approximately 4,000 companies requesting their personnel records. The German government planned to match individuals who met terrorist-threat profiles against the names of those who worked in industries identified as interesting to terrorists, such as airlines and utilities. Few German companies—just 212 out of approximately 4,000—complied with the requests and provided the government with their personnel files. This resistance came despite serious pressure from the government. The BKA ultimately backed down and informed the companies that providing the information would be voluntary.[148] In addition, the German government's ability to obtain financial records remains quite limited even in the course of legally authorized investigations. There exists no central database for private financial accounts, and as a result, German law enforcement officers would have to submit a request to every one of the thousands of banks to ensure that they obtained complete information about a specific individual.[149]

German privacy protections are not limited to personal data. The government's ability to conduct invasive criminal investigations is also limited in other areas, such as wiretapping. In March 2004, the German Constitutional Court ruled that parts of the 1998 wiretapping laws violated aspects of the Basic Law that guaranteed a right to privacy. The 1998 law had allowed police, for the first time, to place bugging devices in homes, subject to court approval. The constitutional court was troubled that these bugs would intercept protected conversations, such as those with close family members, doctors, and religious figures. In order to justify such intrusive surveillance, the court ruled that the government must demonstrate that the crime was "particularly serious" and that the conversation did not deserve protection. The court required the legislature to accommodate this ruling by changing the law within a certain time frame.[150]

As with Germany, British law provided its law enforcement agencies and prosecutors with greater powers, in some areas, than had their counterparts in the United States. Both the 2000 and 2001 antiterrorism acts of Parliament increased the power of both law enforcement and prosecutors—in some ways well beyond the Patriot Act. In fact, a number of the changes made in Britain would likely be deemed unconstitutional in the United States. Again, as with Germany, it is difficult to make broad assessments comparing the changes, because there are also areas in which British legal authorities remain far more constrained than those of the United States.

British law enforcement's ability to stop and search people, without specific suspicion, in designated "Section 44" zones represents a dramatic increase in power, and not surprisingly, has been quite controversial. In the United States, such a law would likely be deemed a violation of the Fourth Amendment to the Constitution. The criminalization of any activity relating to a proscribed organization, including wearing a T-shirt associated with the organization, would also run into constitutional roadblocks in the United States, most likely as a violation of the First Amendment. British legal changes shifting the burden of proof in some terrorist cases from the government to the defendant would likewise be problematic in the United States. From a legislative perspective, however, the most far-reaching British counterterrorism change was not related to law enforcement or prosecutors, but to the government's immigration powers. Part IV of the 2001 act authorized the government to use immigration powers to indefinitely detain in certain circumstances non-British citizens connected to al-Qaeda. This power was later rescinded and replaced with a law granting the government authority to issue "control orders," requiring suspects to remain in a designated area. Both the initial and the more recent legal changes go well beyond any legislative change made by the United States since September 11. Although the United States has taken some extreme measures in the war on terror, such as holding numerous individuals as designated "enemy combatants" without charge, these actions have been taken under the president's executive powers—and have not been based in legislation. In passing the 2001 legislation, the British government explained the need for these powers by noting, "We reluctantly accept that there may be a small category of persons who are suspected international terrorists who cannot be prosecuted, extradited or deported and therefore will have to be detained."[151]

To understand the current state of British law in this area, some background on how the law developed over the past several years is helpful. Part IV of the 2001 Antiterrorism Act allowed the Home Secretary to certify that certain foreign nationals were suspected international terrorists, and to order that they be detained. In most immigration cases, this detention would be followed by a deportation order. However, there are cases in which a person cannot be deported to his home country because of a fear he will be tortured.[152] In these cases, Part IV allowed the British to detain the individual indefinitely. The British have pointed out that these individuals are free to leave at any time, should they find a country willing to accept them. In fact, there were several cases in which detainees left prison after finding countries that would permit them to move there.[153]

Individuals detained under Part IV of the 2001 act were allowed to appeal their detention to the Special Immigration Appeals Commission (SIAC), which would determine, based on all of the available information, whether there existed reasonable grounds for the detention. The suspected terrorists were represented by a security-cleared "special advocate," authorized to view any classified information upon which the detention was based, though the advocates were not permitted to discuss the secret information with their clients.[154] The 2001 act became even more controversial when the SIAC ruled that even evidence obtained via torture in a third country was admissible. The SIAC would consider the fact of torture in weighing evidentiary reliability, but the mere fact that it may have been obtained through torture was not sufficient to exclude it.[155]

Recognizing that this aspect of the law was not compatible with the European Convention for Human Rights (ECHR), Britain applied for a derogation from its obligations, under Article 15(1) of the ECHR, which grants a member state the ability to derogate from the convention in a time of war or public emergency. This derogation was quite controversial, both in Britain and elsewhere in Europe, because the United Kingdom was the only one of the forty-one signatory states that derogated from the ECHR. Nine detainees appealed the legality of the derogation to the SIAC. In July 2002, the SIAC ruled against the detainees, finding that Britain was a likely target of a serious terrorist attack, including one with a weapon of mass destruction. The SIAC also noted that Britain was the United States' closest ally, and that therefore the risk of an attack was so great that the detention powers were necessary.[156] The detainees appealed the decision to the Court of Appeals, which upheld the SIAC's judgment.[157]

The detainees then appealed the legality of their confinement to the Law Lords, the British equivalent of the U.S. Supreme Court. In December 2004, the Law Lords ruled by an eight-to-one majority that British derogation from the ECHR in this case was illegal. The lords found that the law itself was both discriminatory and not proportionate to the threat situation, since it applied only to non-British nationals. They ruled that since the derogation was illegal, the ATCSA was incompatible with Britain's human rights obligations.[158] In response to that ruling, the Home Secretary announced that the British would attempt to replace Part IV with "control orders." These orders would allow the secretary to place a variety of restrictions on the movement, communication, and associations of suspected terrorists against whom there were "grounds for suspicion."[159] These orders, unlike the Part IV authorities, would apply to both British citizens and foreign nationals and would require independent judicial approval.[160] The new proposed legislation also allowed the Home Secretary to impose control orders requiring, in certain circumstances, that an individual remain in one place at all times. This specific type of control order would require derogation from the ECHR as well as parliamentary approval.[161] The Home Secretary noted that while the British government would prefer to prosecute suspected terrorists, there were some cases where this was impossible; the control orders would only be utilized in these unusual cases.[162] In February 2005, the control orders were introduced in Parliament as part of the Prevention of Terrorism legislation. The proposal set off a heated debate, and encountered serious opposition in the House of Lords, whose members demanded that the legislation "sunset" after one year and that the Home Secretary only be allowed to issue control orders when there was the "balance of probability" that the individual was a suspected terrorist.[163]

The debate over this issue took on an increased sense of urgency as March 14, 2005, the date on which the Part IV powers expired, rapidly approached. The issue came to a head when a British judge granted bail to eight of the detainees several days before the expiration date.[164] The legislation was passed soon after, with Prime Minister Blair agreeing to conduct a parliamentary review of the law after one year. The Home Secretary immediately signed control orders for ten of the individuals who had been previously detained at Belmarsh prison. These orders restricted the detainees' access to the internet and cell phones, limited their associates, and imposed a strict curfew. The Home Secretary applied to the High Court to approve these orders, as was required under the new legislation.[165] The individuals subject to the orders were planning to challenge their legality, arguing that they violated human rights law.[166] As of this writing, it remains to be seen whether the various legal challenges will succeed.

While there are areas in which the British legislative changes have gone further than those of the United States in increasing the authority of the government to investigate, prosecute, and detain suspected terrorists, there are also aspects of British counterterrorism law that remain quite restrictive. One unique feature of British law was not changed in any of the post–September 11 legislative packages. Britain remains one of the only democracies in the world in which there is a ban on using intercepted communications in court. There have been repeated proposals over the past ten years to relax this ban, but no immediate change is in sight.[167] While many inside and outside the British government believe that the law should be changed, other influential voices disagree. Notably, the interception commissioner, the individual charged with overseeing the intelligence community's use of its interception authorities, believes that the disadvantages of changing the law would far outweigh the advantages. In his view, putting this information into the public domain will damage the ability of the intelligence services to gather such information in the future. In addition, according to the commissioner, much of the information gathered in this manner is of little use to a jury and would only make sense to someone with a deep knowledge of the subject area.[168] Given his responsibilities and stature, it appears likely that the interception commissioner will prevail in this debate and that the ban will remain intact.

This unique aspect of British law illustrates why it is often so difficult to compare one legal regime to another. Since September 11, pundits throughout the world have opined on how far-reaching the Patriot Act is and the extent to which it infringes on civil liberties. The far more nuanced reality is, unfortunately, not well understood by the public or the media. A more in-depth review reveals that while aspects of the Patriot Act are far-reaching, there are also respects in which other countries such as Britain—and even more surprisingly, Germany—have enacted laws giving their prosecutors and law enforcement officials even greater power.

Notes

1. "Shifting from Prosecution to Prevention, Redesigning the Justice Department to Prevent Future Acts of Terrorism," Department of Justice Fact Sheet, May 29, 2002.

2. Jonathan Stevenson, "Counter-terrorism: Containment and Beyond," *Adelphi Paper* no. 367 (Washington, D.C.: International Institute for Strategic Studies, 2004). Britain and Germany are not alone among European countries in making this shift. A number of other EU states have also adopted a more aggressive law enforcement approach since September 11, preferring to arrest and detain terrorist suspects rather than letting them remain free in the hope of gathering additional intelligence. According to Stevenson, there has been a kind of "bureaucratic peer pressure" in Europe to adopt this more aggressive approach, reflecting an understanding that al-Qaeda-inspired terrorist attacks have the potential to be far more catastrophic than those carried out by the "old-style" terrorist groups active in Europe.

3. Anne Gearan, "U.S. Terror Arrest Tactics Detailed," Associated Press, February 1, 2002.

4. Senior New Scotland Yard official, interview by author, January 2005.

5. Hala Jaber and David Leppard, "Bio-War Suits Found in London Mosque," *Sunday London Times*, January 26, 2003.

6. Robert MacPherson, "Britain Arrests 10 in Anti-Terror Swoop," Agence France Presse, September 30, 2003. The British even simulated a chemical weapons attack in London in September 2003, to ensure that they were prepared in case such an attack actually occurred. See also Stevenson, "Counter-terrorism."

7. For background on this German campaign, see Shawn Boyne, "Law, Terrorism and Social Movements: The Tension between Politics and Security in Germany's Anti-Ter-

rorism Legislation," *Cardozo Journal of International and Comparative Law* 12 (Summer 2004); and James I. Nelson, "Antiterrorismus: The German Experience with Politically Motivated Violence," *Penn State International Law Review* (Spring 2002).

8. Otto Schily (German Interior Minister), "What Can and What Must Germans and Americans Do to Fight Terrorism," speech delivered at closing session of the American-German workshop on cooperation in combating chemical and biological terrorism, February 4, 2003; Ron Niblett and Julianne Smith (of CSIS, interview by author), November 2004. The concern about the possibility of an attack with a weapon of mass destruction is a fairly recent one for the Germans. In 1999, when the Americans started a program to vaccinate the troops against anthrax, for example, the Germans questioned the necessity of the program.

9. "The FBI's Counterterrorism Program since September 2001: Report to the National Commission on Terrorist Attacks upon the United States," April 14, 2004. The FBI previously had a three-tiered system, which it established in 1998. Crimes relating to national or economic security, including terrorism, were considered "Tier 1."

10. 9-11 Commission, *Final Report*, p. 74.

11. "FBI's Counterterrorism Program since September 2001."

12. Ibid. The U.S. Attorney's office in the Southern District of New York prosecuted the 1993 attack upon the World Trade Center; the 1998 bombings of the U.S. embassies in Kenya and Tanzania; the Manila Air case; and the "Landmarks" plots. All of these cases ended with successful prosecutions of the primary perpetrators. These cases were investigated primarily by the New York Office of the FBI. Other FBI field offices and the rest of the law enforcement community were not as focused on the rising Islamic terrorist threat.

13. U.S. Justice Department, *Overview of Information Sharing Initiatives in the War on Terrorism* (Department Fact Sheet, September 19, 2002).

14. Viet Dinh (assistant attorney general), in testimony before the House Judiciary's Subcommittee on the Constitution, May 20, 2003.

15. German government officials, interview by author, December 2004.

16. Peter-Michael Haeberer, interview by author, January, 2005.

17. Francis Miko and Christian Froehlich, *Germany's Role in Fighting Terrorism: Implications for U.S. Policy* (Congressional Research Service, December 27, 2004), p. 4.

18. Boyne, "Law, Terrorism, and Social Movements."

19. Civil Contingencies Secretariat, British Cabinet Office, "Counterterrorism and Resilience: Key Facts," UK Resilience website, September 2004.

20. British Home Office, "One Step Ahead: A 21st Century Strategy to Defeat Organized Criminals," press release (reference 140/2004), March 29, 2004. Available online (www. homeoffice.gov.uk/pageprint.sp?item_id=896).

21. 9-11 Commission, *Final Report*, pp. 327–328. This included arresting individuals under the "material witness statute"—an approach that generated considerable controversy. For example, a judge in New York ruled that the government had no authority to arrest individuals for the purpose of testifying before a grand jury. In her ruling, the judge wrote, "[N]o Congress has granted the government the authority to imprison an innocent person in order to guarantee that he will testify before a grand jury conducting a criminal investigation." See also Phil Hirschkorn, "Judge: Arrest of Sept 11 Witness Was Illegal," CNN, April 30, 2002; available online (http://archives.cnn.com/2002/LAW/04/30/perjury.dismissal/?related).

22. *White House Progress Report in the War on Terror*, September 10, 2003. Available online (www.state.gov/s/ct/rls/rpt/24087.htm).

23. John Ashcroft, "Attorney General Ashcroft Outlines Foreign Terrorist Tracking Task Force" (in speech given at press conference), October 31, 2001.

24. Gearan, "U.S. Terror Arrest Tactics." The ACLU dismissed the argument that this strategy has affected the terrorism statistics. According to the organization, the very low sentences demonstrates that judges—who are free to consider evidence of terrorism not introduced or proved at trial—do not believe that these cases have any terrorism connection. See ACLU, "ACLU Says Skewed Statistics on Terrorism Prosecutions Show Credibility Gap," press release, December 8, 2003; available online (www.aclu.org/safefree/general/16972prs20031208.html).

25. John Soloman, "Terror Suspect Deport Raises Fuss," Associated Press, June 30, 2004. Available online (www.cbsnews.com/stories/2004/06/03/terror/main620825.shtml).

26. "Terrorism Act 2000—Arrest and Charge Statistics," formerly posted on the British Home Office website.

27. "A Mosque Is No Sanctuary," *Guardian* (London), January 21, 2003.

28. "Four More UK Terror Suspects Released," CNN, April 29, 2004.

29. "FBI: NJ al-Qaeda Spy Posed As Student," Associated Press, October 14, 2004.

30. Helen Carter, "Terror Raids, 'Routine' Operation That Ended in Knife Attack," *Guardian* (London), January 15, 2003.

31. "British Security Chiefs Had Intelligence on Splinter Group," BreakingNews.ie, March 30, 2004. Available online (http://archives.tcm.ie/breakingnews/2004/03/30/story140622.asp).

32. "British Judge Grants Terror Suspects Bail," *Guardian* (London), March 11, 2005. Available online (www.guardian.co.uk/worldlatest/story/0,1280,-4858155,00.html).

33. "Profile: Abu Qatada," BBC News, December 7, 2005. Available online (http://news.bbc.co.uk/1/hi/uk/4141594.stm).

34. Robert S. Leiken, *Bearers of Global Jihad? Immigration and National Security After September 11* (Washington, D.C.: The Nixon Center, 2004).

35. British Home Office, "Counter-Terrorism Powers: Reconciling Security and Liberty in an Open Society: A Discussion Paper" (presented to Parliament by the secretary of state), February 2004.

36. "Radical Islamic Extremist Group in Britain Dissolves Itself," Agence France Presse," October 13, 2004.

37. Leiken, *Bearers of Global Jihad?*

38. Lynne O'Donnell, "Militant Muslims Find a Haven in 'Londonistan,'" *San Francisco Chronicle*, July 24, 2004.

39. Leiken, *Bearers of Global Jihad?*

40. Donnell, "Militant Muslims."

41. Peter Clarke, interview by author, January 2005.

42. Leiken, *Bearers of Global Jihad?*

43. Miko and Froehlich, *Germany's Role in Fighting Terrorism*, p. 5; Joint House-Senate September 11 Inquiry, Final Report, p. 186. Prior to September 11, the German government did not devote significant resources to investigating Islamic terrorism, apparently not regarding it as a serious threat.

44. Matthew Schofield, "2 Suspected Terrorists Arrested in Germany," Knight Ridder, January 23, 2005.

45. Craig Whitlock and Shannon Smiley, "Germans Arrest 22 in Anti-Terror Raids," *Washington Post*, January 13, 2005, p. A16.

46. "Germany Nabs Allawi Attack Plot Suspects," Associated Press, December 4, 2004.

47. "Al-Qaeda's New Front: Germany," *Frontline*, January 25, 2005. Available online (www.pbs.org/wgbh/pages/frontline/shows/front/map/de.html).

48. Miko and Froehlich, *Germany's Role in Fighting Terrorism*, pp. 5–6.

49. Ibid., p. 5.

50. Richard Bernstein, "Germany Struggles to Assess True Aims of Islamic Group," *New York Times*, September 26, 2004.

51. Markus Rau, "Country Report: Germany," Max Planck Institute for Comparative Public Law and International Law, n.d.

52. Susan Sachs, "Turkey: Extradited Militant Held on Treason," *New York Times*, October 14, 2004. Available online (http://query.nytimes.com/gst/fullpage.html?res=9401E5DE 163AF937A25753C1A9629C8B63).

53. Oliver Lepsius, "Liberty, Security and Terrorism: The Legal Position in Germany, Part 1 and 2," *German Law Journal* 5, no. 5 (May 2004).

54. "German Court Upholds a Ban on Fund-raising al-Aqsa Foundation," Agence France Presse, December 3, 2004.

55. "Germany Set to Expel Leader of Islamic Foundation," Agence France Presse, May 20, 2005.

56. Jane Kramer, "Germany's Troubled War on Terrorism," *New Yorker*, February 11, 2002.

57. Peter Clare, interview by author, January 2005.

58. "Hundreds Arrested, Few Convicted," BBC News, March 11, 2005. Available online (http://newswww.bbc.net.uk/1/hi/uk/3290383.htm).

59. "Anti-Terror Center Breaks Down Interagency Barriers," *This Week in Germany: Politics*, December 17, 2004.

60. Philip Johnston, "Most Suspects Will Be Free in a Week," *The Daily Telegraph*, August 5, 2004.

61. Peter-Michael Haeberer, interview by author, January 2005; Juergen Maurer (head of counterterrorism for the BKA), interview by author, January 2005. The issue of whether to bring charges in Germany is slightly different from what it is in the United States or Britain. Prosecutors in Germany do not have the same type of prosecutorial discretion as their counterparts in the United States and Britain. If they are aware of a crime, they have to prosecute it. For this reason, prosecutors will sometimes leave meetings if the police and intelligence services are discussing a case in which a crime may have been committed, but in which they are not ready to take action.

62. Details of the law are available on Germany's Federal Ministry of the Interior website (www.zuwanderung.de/english/2_neues-gesetz-a-z/abschiebungsanordnung.html).

63. Breffni O'Rourke, "Europe: Berlin Deports Muslim Cleric As Debate Continues on Anti-Terror Laws," *Radio Free Europe/Radio Liberty*, March 23, 2005.

64. Khaled Schmitt, "Germany to Deport Hundreds of 'Islamists': Report," *IOL*, January 24, 2005.

65. 9-11 Commission, *Final Report*, p. 74.

66. Robert Mueller (FBI Director), in statement before the 9-11 Commission, April 14, 2004.

67. Maurer, interview.

68. See "Anti-Terror Center Breaks Down."

69. Ibid.

70. William Boston, "The Intelligence Test: The Madrid Attacks Spur a Debate on How to Reform Germany's Sprawling Counterterrorism Agencies," *Time*, April 25, 2004; Kramer, "Germany's Troubled War." The federal law enforcement agency's headquarters were in Wiesbaden with the exception of the state security component, which was in Meckenheim. The foreign intelligence service headquarters were in a suburb of Munich. The federal prosecutor was in Karlsruhe, and the domestic intelligence service was in Cologne.

71. "German In-Fighting Threatens EU Terror Initiatives," *Deutsche Welle*, November 5, 2004 (available online at www.dw-world.de/dw/article/0,1564,1386282,00.html); Maurer, interview. For example, should the Germans receive information from a foreign intelligence service that a suspected terrorist was arriving in Germany and would be traveling to many different German states, the federal law enforcement agency could then take charge of the investigation, instead of trying to coordinate between many different states. However, this proposal—which would require a change in law—has generated a backlash and appears unlikely to happen.

72. "Germany to Move Federal Police to Aid Terror Fight," *Deutsche Welle*, January 8, 2004 (available online at www.dw-world.de/dw/article/0,1564,1082139,00.html); "Protestors Call for Resignation of German Federal Police Chief," *Deutsche Welle*, January 17, 2004 (available online at www.dw-world.de/dw/article/0,,1091660,00.html). The move of the BKA to Berlin, for example, prompted protests and rumors that Schily planned to transform the BKA into an organization modeled on the FBI.

73. Craig Horowitz, "The NYPD's War on Terror," *New York*, February 3, 2003. Available online (http://newyorkmetro.com/nymetro/news/features/n_8286).

74. United Nations Security Council, "Fourth Report of UK Pursuant to Resolution 1373," February 23, 2004.

75. See Secret Intelligence Service, United Kingdom, "About Us: SIS in Government" (available online at www.sis.gov.uk/output/Page8.html); Windsor Leadership Trust, "About Us—Trustees: Sir David Omand KCB" (available online at www.windsorleadershiptrust.org.uk/en/1/domand.html).

76. Maurer, interview.

77. Justice Department, "Report from the Field: The USA Patriot Act at Work," July 2004.

78. For detailed discussions regarding the evolution of the "wall," see 9-11 Commission, *Final Report*, pp. 78–80; and the Joint House-Senate September 11 Report, pp. 363–368.

79. Joint House-Senate September 11 Report, p. 365.

80. 9-11 Commission, *Final Report*, pp. 78–79; Justice Department, "Report from the Field." Patrick Fitzgerald, a former federal prosecutor in New York assigned to investigate Osama bin Laden, provided powerful testimony about how this system worked in practice. He noted that he and the FBI criminal investigators could talk to a wide variety of people in the course of their investigation, including private citizens, police officers, foreign intelligence officers, and al-Qaeda members. The only group they could not talk to—because of the "wall"—were FBI agents working on the bin Laden intelligence case.

81. Charles Doyle, *The USA Patriot Act: A Legal Analysis* (Congressional Research Service, April 15, 2002). Consult for a thorough overview of the Patriot Act.

82. United States Foreign Intelligence Surveillance Court of Review, "In re: sealed case No. 02-001," November 18, 2002.

83. Dan Eggen, "Measure Expands Police Powers," *Washington Post*, December 10, 2004.

84. Justice Department, "Report from the Field."

85. Kramer, "Germany's Troubled War." For example, a German intelligence officer complained that "some of our best sources were compromised the minute they became 'visible' to police." This intelligence officer did concede, though, that without better information sharing between intelligence and law enforcement, the Germans were unlikely to be successful in catching terrorists.

86. Clarke, interview.

87. Senior New Scotland Yard official, interview.

88. Nick Davies, "Culture of Muddle Hinders Fight (part 2)," *Guardian* (London), November 10, 2003.

89. Clarke, interview.

90. "Working against Serious Crime," MI-5 (available online at www.mi5.gov.uk/output/page74.html); Edward Alden, Nikki Tait, et al., "Legal Cases in Germany and the U.S. Show How Authorities with Interests That Often Diverge Are Inching towards Greater Co-Operation in Prosecuting Suspects," *Financial Times* (London), October 7, 2004. One official put the date even earlier than that, stating, "The most important date for the (UK) security service is 1992, when MI5 began giving evidence in criminal trials. Almost everything MI5 does has to be done in a form that will not mean it becomes unusable as evidence."

91. Michael Clarke, "Big Shake-up Urged for Prosecution Service," *The Journal* (Newcastle, UK), June 2, 1998.

92. Crown Prosecution Service, *2002–2003 Annual Report*. Available online (www.cps.gov. uk/local/eastern/ar2003herts.html).

93. Jason Bennetto, "Police Link Arrested Student to al-Qa'ida Shoe Bomber," *Independent* (London), November 28, 2003.

94. Helen Carter, "Terror Raids, 'Routine' Operation That Ended in Knife Attack," *Guardian* (London), January 15, 2003.

95. Former MI-5 officer, telephone interview by author, October 8, 2004.

96. Maurer, interview. Maurer believes that the intelligence services will end up changing, culturally, far more than the law enforcement agencies. This cultural change has already begun in his view.

97. Martin Kreickenbaum, "German Interior Ministers End Separation of Police and Intelligence Services," *BORR Terrorism News*, July 20, 2004. The need for the separation between intelligence and law enforcement is based on an April 14, 1949, letter from three Allied countries to the German parliamentary council. In the letter, which outlined the constitutional framework of the new government, the Allies stated that the German intelligence service should not have police powers. The letter is considered to have the force of constitutional doctrine.

98. Kreickenbaum, "German Interior Ministers."

99. "Germany Creates New Terror Center," Deutsche Welle, December 14, 2004 (available online at www.dw-world.de/dw/article/0,1564,1428331,00.html); Maurer, interview.

100. Kreickenbaum, "German Interior Ministers."

101. Maurer, interview.

102. Rainer Grote, "Country Report: United Kingdom," Max Planck Institute for Comparative Public Law and International Law, n.d.

103. FBI, "Legal Attaché Offices: The FBI's International Presence" (available online at www. fbi.gov/contact/legat/legat.htm); Curt Anderson, "FBI Seeking to Expand Presence Overseas to Combat Terrorism," Associated Press, March 28, 2003. For the current figure, see the former source; for the pre–September 11 figure, see the latter source.

104. FBI, "Legal Attaché Offices."

105. Maurer, interview.

106. 9-11 Commission, *Final Report*, p. 81.

107. Joint House-Senate September 11 Inquiry, *Final Report*, p. 90.

108. Robert Mueller, in testimony before the Senate Intelligence Committee, February 16, 2005.

109. German officials, interview by author, December 2004.

110. Maurer, interview; German officials, interview. It should be noted that there are significant differences between the German and U.S. task forces: the German task forces are put together for specific investigations, while the U.S. task forces are permanent structures.

111. Quoted in "Anti-Terrorism, Crime and Security Act 2001," review by Lord Carlile of Berriew, 2004.

112. Helen Fenwick and Colin Warbrick (professors, University of Durham), interview by author, January 10, 2005. One terrorism expert noted that he was startled at the length of the post–September 11 legislation. The 2000 act was so comprehensive that he did not anticipate much more legislation being necessary.

113. Home Office officials, interview by author, January 2005. In the 1990s, the British realized that international terrorism was becoming a major threat, and that their terrorism legislation was only designed to deal with Northern Irish terrorists. The 2000 act was the first time that the British had permanent terrorism legislation in place. Part VII of the act provides temporary measures for Northern Ireland only. These are subject to annual renewal and are time limited to five years. Under the Good Friday Agreement, the British government is committed to the removal of provisions specific to Northern Ireland when the security situation allows.

114. Dinh, testimony. This covered the "pen register" and "trap and trace" techniques, which allow the government to track the numbers—but not the content—of phone calls made and received.

115. Michael Woods, "Counterintelligence and Access to Transactional Records: A Practical History of USA Patriot Act Section 215," *Journal of National Security Law and Policy* 1 no. 1 (2005). Consult for a very detailed discussion of National Security Letters.

116. Dinh, testimony. Still, as former assistant attorney general Viet Dinh pointed out, the words "library" and "bookstore" do not appear in the Patriot Act.

117. Senator Jon Kyl, "Amending the FISA Law," in speech before U.S. Senate, October 15, 2002 (available online at www.fas.org/irp/congress/2002_cr/s101502.html); Bob Barr (American Conservative Union), in testimony before the House Subcommittee on Crime, Terrorism, and Homeland Security, May 18, 2004. This amendment, which was first put forth by Senators Kyl and Charles Schumer has been frequently referred to as the "Moussaoui fix." Others, such as Bob Barr, dispute that the Moussaoui situation illustrated the need for this change.

118. "Ashcroft Testifies Regarding PATRIOT Act," *Tech Law Journal*, June 8, 2004 (available online at www.techlawjournal.com/topstories/2004/20040608.asp); David Johnston and James Risen, "U.S. Agencies Warn Attack on Iraq Will Unleash Acts of Terror," *New York Times*, February, 22, 2003.

119. While this provision will certainly increase the FBI's ability to target suspected terrorists, it is unclear whether it will survive judicial review. Civil liberties groups argue that the measure violates Fourth Amendment protections against unreasonable search and seizure. Hence, the issue will likely end up in the courts, presumably once the Justice Department attempts to prosecute an individual on whom they obtained a FISA warrant using this provision. The defendant, however, will likely be in the awkward position of having to challenge the legality of the FISA warrant without knowing whether the department relied on the "lone wolf" provision in the FISA application.

120. Dinh, testimony.

121. Alan Travis, "Police to Get Extra Week to Question Terror Suspects," *Guardian* (London), May 12, 2003.

122. "Anti-Terrorism, Crime, and Security Act 2001 Review: Report, Privy Counselor Review Committee," December 18, 2003.

123. Grote, "Country Report: United Kingdom."

124. "Report on the Operation in 2002 and 2003 of the Terrorism Act 2000," Lord Carlile of Berriew, Q.C., citing R (on the application of Gillan) v. 1) Commissioner of Police of the Metropolis, 2) the secretary of state for the Home Department: R (on the application of Quinton) v. Same (2003) DC (Brooke LJ, Marucie Kay J), October 31, 2003. A suit was filed challenging the blanket authorization for the city of London and the use of the Section 44 powers at an East London arms fair. The court held that the rolling authorizations in London were justified by the terrorist threat. In terms of the arms fair itself, the court found that this was a "close call," but that in the end the powers were appropriate for this situation.

125. "Anti-Terrorism, Crime, and Security Act 2001 Review."

126. Grote, "Country Report."

127. Miko and Froehlich, *Germany's Role in Fighting Terrorism*; Lepsius, "Liberty, Security, and Terrorism." Some have noted that the legal changes after September 11 were only partially precipitated by the terrorist attacks. As with provisions in the Patriot Act, a number of these measures adopted in Germany were already under consideration before the attacks.

128. Lepsius, "Liberty, Security, and Terrorism."

129. Ibid.

130. Steve Gold, "German Carriers Told to Install Cyber-Snooping Tech," *Newsbytes*, October 25, 2001.

131. Haeberer, interview.

132. Justice Department, "Report from the Field."

133. 9-11 Commission, *Final Report*, p. 67. The new IRTPA provision is particularly significant in light of U.S. intelligence estimates that 10,000–20,000 individuals received training at al-Qaeda camps in Afghanistan from 1996 to 2001, in addition to the many individuals who attended training camps run by other terrorist organizations. In addition, IRTPA clarifies portions of the material support statute that some federal courts have found unconstitutional. For example, in *Humanitarian Law Project, et al. v. John Ashcroft, et al.*, the plaintiffs sought to provide assistance to the Kurdistan Workers Party (PKK) and the Liberation Tigers of Tamil Eelam (LTTE), both of which had been designated as terrorist organizations by the U.S. government. In January 2004, a federal court in California agreed with the plaintiffs that the phrase "expert advice and assistance" was impermissibly vague and thus violated the First Amendment. See *Humanitarian Law Project v. Ashcroft*, 309 F.Supp.2d 1185. In 1998, the plaintiffs had brought a similar suit arguing that the "training" and "personnel" terms in the material support statute were unconstitutionally vague; in a December 2003 decision, the 9th Circuit Court agreed with them. *Humanitarian Law Project v. Reno*, 205 F.3d 1130 (9th Cir., 2000). Yet another part of the statute was deemed unconstitutional by a federal judge in New York in July 2003. Ahmed Sattar and other followers of the "Blind Sheikh" Omar Abdul Rahman had been charged under the measure barring provision of communications equipment for allegedly transmitting information from the imprisoned sheikh to other members of the Egyptian al-Gamaa al-Islamiya (the Islamic Group) worldwide. In dismissing two counts of the indictment, however, the court found that the term "communications equipment" was unconstitutionally vague. *United States v. Sattar*, 272 F.Supp.2d 1185 (C.D. Cal., 2004). IRTPA addressed the courts' decisions by including more detailed definitions of the terms "training," "expert advice or assistance," and "knowingly provided."

134. Miko and Froehlich, *Germany's Role in Fighting Terrorism*.

135. Grote, "Country Report"; Lord Carlile of Berriew, Q.C., "Report on the Operation in 2002 and 2003 of the Terrorism Act 2000." According to Lord Carlile, the Special Branch officers had mixed feelings about proscription. While these tools are important, keeping track of all of the proscribed groups was described as a difficult task. Moreover, groups are often able to change their names to avoid proscription.

136. Carlile, "Report." For example, four organizations were added to the list on November 1, 2002.

137. "Reconciling Security and Liberty in an Open Society," *Liberty*, August 2004.

138. Ibid.

139. Grote, "Country Report."

140. Carlile, "Report."

141. "Reconciling Security and Liberty."

142. Rau, "Country Report: Germany." The legality of the grid searches has been challenged since September 11 in a number of German states. Most courts have upheld the technique as legal.

143. Otto Schily (Federal Minister of the Interior), "What Can and What Must Germans and Americans Do to Fight Terrorism," speech, Washington, D.C., February 4, 2003.

144. Haeberer, interview. One LKA identified "interesting" people through its profiling efforts, some of whom were engaged in criminal activity, but no terrorists. Other LKAs had similar experiences.

145. Susan Cornwell, "Senate Blocks Funding for Pentagon Database," Reuters, January 23, 2003; Stevenson, "Counter-terrorism." Interestingly, there were, in fact, some privacy protections built into the system. For example, if the program detected suspicious activity by a particular individual, the individual's name would be blocked out until the government had received judicial approval. However, these protections were apparently of limited comfort to the senators, and they received little attention during the debate over TIA.

146. Ian Johnson and David Crawford, "Germany's Terrorist Hunt Spurs Corporate Defiance," *Wall Street Journal*, August 9, 2002.

147. "PHR2004—Federal Republic of Germany," *Privacy International*, November 16, 2004.

148. Johnson and Crawford, "Germany's Terrorist Hunt."

149. Kramer, "Germany's Troubled War."

150. "PHR2004—Federal Republic of Germany."

151. Tom Parker, "Preventive Detention in the United Kingdom, Citing Home Affairs Committee, First Report Session 2000–2001: Terrorism, Crime, and Security Bill 2001—Counterterrorism Policies in the United Kingdom," in Philip Heymann and Juliette Kayyem, eds., *Protecting Liberty in an Age of Terror* (Cambridge: Massachusetts Institute of Technology, 2005).

152. "Counter-Terrorism Powers: Reconciling Security and Liberty in an Open Society: A Discussion Paper," British Home Office, February 2004. Article 3 of the European Convention on Human Rights and the relevant case law prohibits the deportation of individuals to countries where they might be tortured. The French have interpreted this law far more liberally than the British. For the French, for example, a guarantee from the Algerian government that it will not torture an extradited individual has been

sufficient to allow for deportation. The British, on the other hand, are not willing to accept this guarantee at face value. Therefore, there may be situations in which the French would consider it legal to deport an individual to Algeria but where the British would find it illegal.

153. See "Reconciling Security and Liberty." The civil liberties group Liberty pointed out the problems with this policy in terms of its effectiveness in combating terrorism. For example, one detainee who was both a French and Algerian citizen was able to leave prison and return to France. The British police took this detainee on the Eurostar and dropped him off in Paris. As Liberty states, "If he was an international terrorist, this cannot be an effective way of safeguarding national security."

154. "Anti-Terrorism, Crime, and Security Act 2001 Review: Report, Privy Counselor Review Committee," December 18, 2003. The SIAC is an independent judicial entity that was established in 1997 for the purpose of hearing immigration-related appeals.

155. "Review of Counterterrorism Powers," Session 2003–2004, House of Lords, House of Commons, Joint Committee on Human Rights, July 21, 2004.

156. Grote, "Country Report."

157. "Review of Counterterrorism Powers."

158. "Opinion of the Lords of Appeal for Judgment in the Cause of A (FC) and others (FC) (Appellants) v. Secretary of State for the Home Department," December 16, 2004.

159. Alan Cowell, "Bitter Political Duel in Britain over New Anti-Terror Legislation," *New York Times*, March 9, 2005.

160. According to a "Frequently Asked Questions" section formerly posted on the Home Office website (www.homeoffice.gov.uk).

161. British Home Office, "Security and Liberty-Home Secretary Published Balanced Measures," press release (reference 034/2005), February 22, 2005.

162. Ibid.

163. Cowell, "Bitter Political Duel."

164. "British Judge Grants Terror Suspects Bail," *Guardian* (London), March 11, 2005. Available online (www.guardian.co.uk/worldlatest/story/0,1280,-4858155,00.html).

165. "Ten Receive 'Terrorism' Control Orders under New British Rules," *Khaleej Times*, March 12, 2005.

166. Robert Verkaik, "Terror Suspects' Lawyers Challenge Control Orders," *New Zealand Herald*, March 15, 2005. Available online (www.nzherald.co.nz/index.cfm?c_id=2&ObjectID=10115369).

167. Joint Committee on Human Rights, *Review of Counterterrorism Powers*, July 21, 2004.

168. Sir Swinton Thomas (Interception Commissioner), interview by author, January, 2005.

Mixed Results with the Preventive Approach

IT HAS BEEN DIFFICULT TO GAUGE THE SUCCESS OF THE U.S. shift in counterterrorism strategy since September 11 toward a more preemptive approach. The topic has been the subject of heated rhetoric from all sides. The Justice Department maintains that it has been incredibly successful in both preventing attacks—noting that none have occurred in the United States since September 11—and in prosecuting suspected terrorists. In July 2004, for example, the Justice Department released a paper titled "Report from the Field: Patriot Act at Work." Intended to boost support for the Patriot Act, the report claimed that of the 310 individuals charged since September 11 in terrorism cases, 179 had been convicted.[1] In announcing these figures, Attorney General John Ashcroft referred to the Patriot Act as "al-Qaeda's worst nightmare."[2] On the other hand, the Justice Department's critics claim that the department has exaggerated the terrorist threat, selectively targeted and prosecuted Muslims, and had few, if any, successes in prosecuting actual terrorists.[3] Critics have frequently pointed to a spate of reports since September 11 charging that the Justice Department has inflated statistics to create an appearance of counterterrorism success.[4]

The reality is, not surprisingly, somewhere in between. Overall, the Justice Department has had a very mixed record in this arena since September 11.[5] While the department has had some important counterterrorism successes, including both judge and jury convictions and plea bargains resulting in long sentences, it has also discovered that the paradigm shift from reaction to prevention is a very difficult challenge. There have been cases in which defendants have been acquitted of terrorism charges, where convictions have been later overturned, and where terrorism charges have been dropped.

It has likewise been difficult to gauge the success of British and German prosecutors and law enforcement agencies in their preventive counterterrorism efforts, but for different reasons. While Britain and Germany have arrested and charged hundreds of individuals in the course of counterterrorism investigations since September 11, many of these cases are still proceeding slowly through the respective systems and have not been resolved. What is clear from those cases that have been concluded, however, is that each country—Germany even more so than Britain—has had a very mixed record since September 11 in targeting suspected terrorists. There have been cases in which both countries have successfully prosecuted dangerous individuals clearly affiliated with Islamic terrorist organizations, but in many other cases the outcome was far less successful.[6]

Successful Prosecutions

The United States, Germany, and Britain have each had important terrorism-related convictions since September 11. The United States boasts by far the largest number of convictions, with almost 200 as of July 2004, according to the Justice Department. While critics have challenged both the number and the quality of these convictions, the fact remains that there have been many successful counterterrorism prosecutions. The British have had fewer—but not a few—successes, with 17 individuals convicted under the 2000 Terrorism Act by December 2004.[7] Germany does not release comparable terrorism statistics, which makes a direct comparison more difficult. While the number of successful prosecutions in Germany appears to be far lower than in either the United States or Britain, the Germans have had at least several important convictions in cases related to Islamic terrorism.

The United States has obtained both judge and jury convictions in a number of terrorism cases since September 11. In April 2005, for example, Ali al-Timimi, a Virginia imam, was convicted by a jury on all ten counts relating to his inciting supporters to prepare for jihad against the United States. Less than a week after the September 11 attacks, Timimi preached to his supporters that "the time had come for them to go abroad and join the mujahideen engaged in violent jihad in Afghanistan."[8] A month before Timimi's conviction, a New York jury convicted Yemeni Sheikh Muhammad Ali Hasan al-Moayad and his assistant Muhammad Mohsen Yahya Zayed of conspiring to provide material support to both Hamas and al-Qaeda, including help with fundraising and financing.[9] American juries have also found other defendants guilty of terrorism-related charges, including Lynn Stewart. Stewart was the lawyer for Omar Abdel Rahman, also known as the "Blind Sheikh"; she was convicted of material support for terrorism for facilitating communication between the prison-bound Sheikh and his followers.[10]

The United States obtained judicial convictions against three of the defendants in the so-called "Virginia jihad" case. They and eight other defendants were charged on a variety of counts for their alleged preparation for holy war. Three of the defendants believed they could not get a fair jury trial in northern Virginia, and waived their Constitutional right to a jury trial.[11] The federal judge who therefore heard the case convicted the three men on a variety of charges, including conspiracy to levy war against the United States, and conspiracy to provide material support to the Taliban and Lashkar-e-Taiba.[12]

In addition to the successes in the courtroom, the United States has reached plea agreements with a number of defendants in terrorism cases, many of whom were subsequently sentenced to lengthy prison terms. Among these are:

- "Shoe bomber" Richard Reid, who was sentenced to life in prison for attempting to blow up an American Airlines jet during a flight from Paris to Miami;

- Six U.S. citizens in Lackawanna, New York—better known as the "Lackawanna Six"—who trained in al-Qaeda camps in the spring and summer of 2001, and were sentenced to prison terms of between seven and ten years after pleading guilty to terrorism-related charges, and;

- Iyman Faris, the Ohio truck driver who pleaded guilty and was sentenced to twenty years in prison for scouting out potential U.S. targets for al-Qaeda.[13]

The British have also obtained jury convictions in several prosecutions of Islamist terrorists. In April 2005, after a lengthy trial that cost an estimated twenty million pounds, a jury convicted suspected terrorist Kamel Bourgass.[14] Bourgass, an al-Qaeda-trained Algerian, was found guilty of murdering the policeman he stabbed during a police raid, and also of conspiracy to cause public nuisance with explosives or poison. The jury could not reach a verdict on the charge of conspiracy to murder.[15] After the final verdict, the judge stated, "Had the operation come to fruition, the resulting fear and disrupting with the potential for injury and widespread panic would have been substantial."[16] Bourgass conceded during the trial that he had helped another individual write the poison recipe found by police in a London apartment, but said that it was intended for use by villagers in Algeria in the event that they were attacked by terrorist groups.[17] The jury did not believe Bourgass's claims and he was sentenced to life imprisonment for stabbing the policeman—and received an additional seventeen years for his involvement in the poison plot.[18] As will be discussed later, however, this case was far from a complete success, as the British prosecutors failed to bring charges against Bourgass's eight co-defendants.

The British were also successful in prosecuting a radical cleric for inciting violence. Sheikh Abdullah el-Faisal, an associate of notorious Islamist imam Abu Hamza al-Masri, frequently gave inflammatory speeches in which he told his supporters that it was their duty to kill Americans, Jews, and Hindus. El-Faisal also supported the use of chemical weapons in the context of jihad. He was charged for soliciting murder, and was convicted by a jury in March 2003 and sentenced to nine years in prison.[19]

At least one terrorist in Britain with ties to al-Qaeda also pleaded guilty for his role in a terrorist plot.[20] Sajid Badat, a British-born Muslim who was an associate of shoe bomber Richard Reid, pleaded guilty to conspiring to blow up an aircraft. Underscoring the significance of the case, the British press referred to the trial as the "first major prosecution of an al-Qa'ida associate in the UK since 9/11." Like Reid, Badat had apparently also planned to blow up a U.S.-bound plane with a shoe bomb, but changed his mind several days before the scheduled date and withdrew from the operation. British authorities believe that Badat became radicalized in the late 1990s at a London mosque and then spent two years in Afghanistan at al-Qaeda training camps before returning to Britain.[21]

Germany does not use a jury system, but has also obtained some judicial convictions in post–September 11 prosecutions of Islamist terrorists. In November 2003, Shadi Abdallah, a twenty-seven-year-old Palestinian born in Jordan, was sentenced to a four-year prison term by a German court. Abdallah, who was arrested by German authorities in April 2002, confessed that he was a member of Abu Musab al-Zarqawi's al-Tawhid organization. He also acknowledged that he and other Tawhid members had planned to attack Jewish targets in Germany. In fact, when he entered Germany, in preparation for the attacks, Abdallah brought with him hand grenades and a gun with a silencer. Abdallah also testified that he had spent time at al-Qaeda's training camps in Afghanistan, where he received military and terrorist training, and even served as bin Laden's bodyguard for several weeks. Trials against other Tawhid members in Germany are still pending as of this writing.[22]

The Germans also successfully prosecuted four individuals arrested before September 11 for terrorist activity. These Algerian individuals were arrested in December 2000 and charged with plotting to attack targets at the Christmas Market in Strasbourg, France. During a search of the suspects' apartment, police found a cache of weapons, chemicals, and detonators. In March 2003, a German court found the four guilty of conspiracy to commit murder and carry out a bombing. They were sentenced to prison terms of ten and twelve years.[23] The case was not a complete success, however; one of their associates, Boudid-Abdelkader O, was tried separately and acquitted.

Even in many of their successful terrorism prosecutions, the United States, Germany, and Britain encountered serious problems, difficulties that illustrate how challenging it can be to prove terrorism-related charges in the criminal justice context.

For example, British authorities arrested two Algerians soon after September 11, charging them with a variety of offenses, including terrorism- and nonterrorism-related crimes. The terrorism charges were for offenses named under the Terrorism Act 2000: specifically, being a member of a proscribed organization and raising funds for terrorist organizations. The two Algerians moved to Britain in 1997 and began recruiting young British Muslims for the jihad, helping them travel to Afghanistan for training. The two also raised money for al-Qaeda through a credit card fraud scheme and provided other logistical support for potential operatives, including false passports and other documentation. The prosecution decided, however, to drop the terrorism charge of membership in a proscribed organization after determining that it would be too difficult to prove. Al-Qaeda, the prosecutors noted, did not have a command structure, as did groups like the IRA. The prosecutors proceeded on the terrorism-financing charges and on some of the more minor criminal charges, such as credit card and passport fraud.[24]

The two men were ultimately convicted of these charges and sentenced to eleven years in prison. Terrorism expert Rohan Gunaratna stated that despite the conviction, dropping the membership charge was a "major blow" and added, "What's the point of all of this effort to draft a new terrorism act if they can't deal with terrorists who they want to prosecute?"[25]

There have also been successful terrorism prosecutions in the United States in which some of the terrorism charges have been dropped or dismissed. For example, in the Virginia jihad case, the judge dismissed against defendant Hammad Abdur-Raheem a charge that he had assisted the other defendants in training in Pakistan, since Abdur-Raheem himself had not actually trained there. In dismissing the charge, the judge stated that the links prosecutors tried to prove were "too disconnected."[26] Abdur-Raheem was still convicted on another three counts, including conspiring to provide material support to Lashkar-e-Taiba, conspiracy, and firearms conspiracy.[27]

The case of suspected September 11 conspirator Zacarias Moussaoui provides the most valuable example of how difficult it can be to prosecute suspected terrorists, even in cases with successful outcomes. On August 15, 2001, the FBI initiated an investigation of Moussaoui, a flight student in Minnesota. An FBI agent discovered that Moussaoui had jihadist beliefs and that he could not provide a plausible explanation for the origin of the $32,000 in his bank account. The agent concluded that Moussaoui was an "Islamic extremist preparing for some future act in furtherance of radical fundamental goals." The INS detained Moussaoui on immigration grounds, and a deportation order was signed on August 17, 2001.[28] Moussaoui was indicted on December 11, 2001, and charged with six separate counts relating to his alleged participation in the September 11 attacks.[29] Moussaoui, according to the indictment, followed many of the same patterns and took many of the same steps as the hijackers themselves.[30] In April 2005—more than three-and-a-half years after he was first arrested—Moussaoui pleaded guilty to all six counts, including conspiracy to commit acts of terrorism transcending national boundaries, conspiracy to commit aircraft piracy, and conspiracy to use weapons of mass destruction.[31]

As is discussed at greater length below, during the course of the three-and-a-half-year litigation, Moussaoui managed to tie the system in knots, with the proceedings including numerous appeals by both him and the U.S. government on a variety of different issues. The most time-consuming and difficult issue was Moussaoui's requests for access to captured al-Qaeda members. This issue is at the heart of the difficulties in prosecuting suspected terrorists. It raises two important constitutional issues—a defendant's right to a fair trial, and the government's need to be able to fight terrorism effectively. Balancing these two interests is an extremely difficult challenge, as became clear at many points during the Moussaoui litigation.

Less Successful Prosecutions

While the difficulty of prosecuting suspected terrorists is even evident from some of the cases with successful outcomes, the obstacles have been far more clear in the many terrorism prosecutions in which the United States, Germany, and Britain have not ultimately succeeded. The results in these cases have varied widely, and it is hardly accurate to categorize all of them as "failures." In some of these cases, the government in question was still able to obtain convictions for nonterrorism-related crimes, while in others the prosecution failed entirely and the defendants were ultimately acquitted on all counts. There have also been apparent successes in which convictions on terrorism-related charges have later been overturned. Finally, in many cases, the government did not even bring charges against individuals initially arrested for terrorism-related activity. The following sections explore cases whose outcomes have been less than successful.

Acquittals on all charges. In the United States, both juries and judges have acquitted Islamic terror suspects of all charges in several high-profile cases. For example, an Idaho jury acquitted of all charges Sami Omar al-Hussayen, a Saudi graduate student in the United States who had been charged with conspiracy to provide material support of resources to Hamas and other violent jihadists. The government alleged that al-Hussayen created and operated websites on behalf of the Islamic Assembly of North America (ISNA), and two radical Saudi sheikhs. Al-Hussayen, according to the indictment, knew that his computer services would be used to raise funds for the jihad in Israel, Chechnya, and elsewhere and "conspired to conceal the nature of his activities." Al-Hussayen was also charged with moderating an e-mail group for people interested in participating in the violent jihad, and with providing money and equipment to Hamas.[32]

In announcing the indictment of al-Hussayen on terrorism-related charges, Ashcroft stated that the case would provide Americans with a glimpse of the terrorist threat, a threat Ashcroft said "[is] fanatical, and it is fierce."[33] The case started out strong. In the opening arguments, the federal prosecutor portrayed al-Hussayen to the jury as someone with a "dual persona: one face to the public and a private face of extreme jihad." Following the trial, one juror told the *Seattle Times* that after the opening statements he thought to himself that al-Hussayen would be in jail for life.[34] The case quickly unraveled. At one point, the judge threw out some of the government's evidence tying al-Hussayen to ISNA, subsequently warning the prosecutors that he would dismiss the case unless they could clearly demonstrate that al-Hussayen was responsible for the "terrorist" material on the websites. The judge also told the prosecutors, "When you make broad assertions to this court, make sure you know what you're talking about."[35] Al-Hussayen was ultimately acquitted of all charges against him. In this case, at least one juror made clear that he considered the verdict a complete vindication for al-Hussayen, stating after the case that "there was not a word spoken that indicated he supported terrorism. . . . It was a real stretch."[36]

A jury also acquitted one of the defendants of all charges in the Detroit "sleeper cell" case, which is considered at greater length below. Farouk Ali-Hamoud had been charged for his alleged participation in a terrorist conspiracy and also with document fraud.[37] Another defendant, Ahmed Hannan, was acquitted of the terrorism charge, but convicted for the non-terrorism-related offense of document fraud. Two other defendants were convicted on both terrorism and nonterrorism-related charges, but as will be discussed later, their convictions were later overturned.[38]

A federal judge, and not a jury, acquitted one of the "Virginia jihad" members of terrorism charges. Sabri Benkhala was charged with supplying services to the Taliban by virtue of his fighting in Afghanistan, but was ultimately acquitted. In acquitting Benkhala, the judge in the case made clear that she did not believe that the prosecutors had proved that the defendant was guilty of the terrorism-related charges.[39] The case against another one of the Virginia jihad members did not even make it that far. Caliph Basha Ibn Abdur-Raheem had faced charges of conspiracy and firearms violations for his alleged activities in connection with Lashkar-e-Taiba. The judge threw out the charges against Abdur-Raheem before trial, saying that there was no evidence that he was preparing for jihad, as the prosecutors had alleged.[40]

The United States encountered similar difficulties with another terrorism prosecution. Two individuals in Albany, New York—Yassin Aref and Mohammed Hossain—were arrested on charges of conspiracy, money laundering, and providing material support to terrorism. Aref was the imam of a mosque in Albany, while Hossain was one of the mosque's founders. According to the indictment, the two attempted to purchase a shoulder-fired missile that would then have been used to assassinate Pakistan's ambassador to the United Nations.[41] The government successfully argued after their arrest that the two should be denied bail, in part because an address book had been found in an Iraqi terrorist camp that included a reference in Arabic to Aref as "the commander." The government later acknowledged that a mistake had been made in the translation and that the word in the address book was actually Kurdish, not Arabic, and meant "brother" and not "commander." In response to this revelation, the judge ordered the two released from jail, and instead made them subject to home arrest. In issuing this ruling, the judge made clear that his views on the case had changed significantly. The judge stated that "the evidence in this case appears less strong today" and that there was no evidence to support the U.S. government's contention that either of the two defendants had terrorist ties.[42]

The British have also had a number of defendants acquitted of all counts in terrorism prosecutions. In one of the most severe and highly publicized blows to British counterterrorism efforts, in April 2005 eight out of nine terrorist suspects were cleared of terrorism-related charges. The only person convicted was Kamel Bourgass, who, as discussed above, was convicted for fatally stabbing a police officer during the raid, and for terrorism-related offenses. British police arrested in January 2003 the nine original defendants—including Bourgass—after receiving a tip that one of these individuals was planning to plant poison in various locations around London. During one of the raids conducted in the course of this investigation, police found recipes and the ingredients for making a variety of poisons, including anthrax and cyanide. Police also discovered instructions on how to transform the poisons into a more lethal gaseous form. Government scientists stated that though no actual poison was found in the house, the evidence demonstrated in their view that efforts had been made to produce a poison. When applying the discovered recipes, scientists were able to produce enough poison to kill hundreds of people.[43] Despite the scientific testimony, a jury acquitted four of the defendants, and prosecutors subsequently decided to drop the charges against the other four defendants.[44]

The British also failed in their efforts to convict three defendants in a case stemming from a suicide attack on a bar in Tel Aviv by two British citizens. During their post-attack investigation, the British police discovered that one of the bombers had sent his wife in Britain an e-mail stating, "We did not spend a long time together in this world but I hope through Allah's mercy ... we can spend eternity together." Based largely on this communication, the British charged the bomber's wife, brother, and sister for failing to report information that might have prevented a terrorist attack—an offense included in the 2000 Terrorism Act. The wife claimed that she did not know what her husband was planning, and that she believed that her husband was merely letting her know in the e-mail that he was leaving her. Ultimately, the wife was acquitted, and jurors could not agree on a verdict for the brother and sister. The British government planned to retry the brother and sister on the same charges.[45]

Finally, in August 2002, a British jury acquitted Sulayman-ul-Abidin of terrorism charges, in a case with similarities to the al-Hussayen prosecution in Idaho. Abidin was arrested several weeks after the September 11 attacks for running a website that prosecutors claimed was a recruiting effort for the jihad. The site, called the "Ultimate Jihad Challenge," which advertised itself as "Britain's first Islamic threat assessment unit," offered a two-week firearms training course in the United States. The government became even more suspicious of Abidin when articles about al-Qaeda and bin Laden were discovered in a search of his laptop computer. Abidin disputed the government's contention that he was supporting terrorism, arguing that he was merely running a security service. A jury agreed with Abidin, acquitting him on all charges.[46]

In Germany as well, multiple terrorist suspects have been acquitted of all counts after lengthy trials. The highest profile case involved "Hamburg cell" associate Abdelghani Mzoudi. In May 2003, Mzoudi was charged for his alleged role in the September 11 attacks. He was charged with being an accessory to murder and with membership in a terrorist organization. The prosecutor's office, in a released statement, argued that Mzoudi was involved in the preparation of the attacks and had also helped the cell members conceal their travel.[47] Toward the end of the trial, however, the BKA—as required by law—reported to the court a piece of what it deemed to be exculpatory evidence.[48] The BKA report said that there was credible intelligence from an "unidentified informer" that out of the Hamburg group, only hijackers Mohammed Atta, Marwan al-Shehhi, Ziad Jarrah, and facilitator Ramzi Binalshib were involved in the planning of the attack. According to this source, the four of them did not talk to any others—including Mzoudi—about actual terrorist operations. Based on this report, the court released Mzoudi from custody and he was later acquitted of the charges against him.[49]

As was mentioned earlier, one of the defendants in the Strasbourg Christmas market case was also acquitted of terrorism offenses. A Frankfurt court found Algerian Boudid-Abdelkader O innocent of membership in a terrorist group. The case against him was plagued by problems from the outset, and the eventual outcome was not surprising. He had initially been jointly charged with the other defendants for planning the attack on the Christmas market. When the prosecutors realized that it would be difficult to prove his complicity in the attack, they decided to try him separately from the other defendants. The prosecution then reduced the charges against him, dropping the allegation that he had assisted in the planning of the attack and charging him only with prior knowledge of the plot. He was eventually acquitted by the court of this charge as well.[50]

Success with prosecuting nonterrorism offenses. In many other cases, Germany, Britain, and the United States have failed to prove terrorism charges, but have succeeded on other grounds. An example of such a case in the United States was the prosecution of Enaam Arnaout, director of Benevolence International Foundation (BIF), a nongovernmental organization incorporated in 1992 in Illinois and describing itself as "devoted to relieving the suffering of Muslims around the world." BIF received, according to its IRS filing, more than $15 million in donations from 1995 to 2000. Enaam Arnaout became the director of BIF in 1993.[51]

The FBI began investigating BIF in 1998, based on foreign intelligence reports that Arnaout was providing logistical support for jihadists. By September 11, FBI agents believed that BIF had ties to al-Qaeda and was supporting jihad (though the agents did not believe at the time that they could prove a criminal case against either Arnaout or BIF). On December 14, 2001, the Treasury Department's Office of Foreign Assets Control (OFAC) froze BIF's assets, using a provision of the Patriot Act that allowed the government to do so, during the "pendency of an investigation." That same day, the FBI conducted a search of BIF offices in Chicago.[52] Arnaout was indicted by a grand jury in October 2002 and charged with several criminal counts, including conspiracy to provide material support to terrorists, money laundering, wire and mail fraud, and conspiracy to engage in a racketeering enterprise. In a Chicago press conference announcing the indictment, Attorney General Ashcroft stated that Arnaout was accused of concealing from the government and others his relationship with al-Qaeda, Osama bin Laden, and other terrorist organizations. Ashcroft noted, "It is chilling that the origins of al-Qaeda were discovered in a charity claiming to do good," adding that "it is sinister to prey on good hearts to fund the works of evil." Ashcroft went on to say, "There is no moral distinction between those who carry out terrorist attacks and those who knowingly finance terrorist attacks." He vowed that the U.S. government would find the sources of "terrorist blood money" and shut them down.[53]

Arnaout ultimately pleaded guilty to conspiracy to engage in racketeering—a serious, but nonterrorism-related felony charge. The government asked the court, however, to apply the terrorist sentencing guidelines, which would have resulted in a far longer sentence. In denying the government's request, the court noted, "Arnaout does not stand convicted of a terrorist offense. Nor does the record reflect that he attempted, participated in, or conspired to commit any act of terrorism."[54]

In Germany, a suspected Islamic terrorist named Ihsan Garnaoui was acquitted of terrorism charges after a lengthy trial, but was convicted of other offenses. Garnaoui was arrested in Germany on March 20, 2003, the first day of the war in Iraq. The timing of the arrest was not a coincidence, as prosecutors believed that Garnaoui was planning attacks for when the long-anticipated war would begin.[55] During a search of Garnaoui's apartment, German investigators found computer files with detailed bomb-making diagrams, as well as materials that they believed could have served as timers for a bomb.[56] Garnaoui was accused of attending an al-Qaeda training camp in Afghanistan, and of recruiting individuals in Berlin to carry out attacks against Jewish and U.S. targets in Germany.[57] Though ultimately convicted of illegal weapons possession and tax evasion, Garnaoui was acquitted of terrorism-related charges.[58] Prosecutors announced that they would appeal the decision.

Overturned convictions. Both Germany and the United States have had terrorism convictions overturned. The example in the United States occurred in the Detroit "sleeper cell" case, in which five defendants were originally charged with operating as a "covert underground support unit for terrorist attacks," as well as a "sleeper" operational cell. They were accused of conspiring to provide material support and resources to those plotting to conduct terrorist attacks in Jordan, Turkey, and the United States. These charges were based on documents found by the FBI in the defendants' possession, including airport identification badges, other false identification, and a day planner that contained references to the "American base in Turkey," the "American foreign minister," and "Alia airport" in Jordan. This day planner also included sketches of what an FBI agent said appeared to be an airport flight line.[59]

The case received a great deal of media and public attention, in part because of comments from top U.S. officials. Attorney General Ashcroft began promoting this case soon after the initial arrests were made in September 2001. At a press conference in October 2001, Ashcroft said that the men were "suspected of having knowledge" of the September 11 attacks—a charge that was quickly withdrawn.[60] During the trial, Ashcroft praised a government witness in the case on at least two occasions, referring to his cooperation as a "critical tool" in the war on terror.[61] The case received even more attention when President Bush himself pointed to it (following the convictions of two of the defendants on terrorism charges) as an example of an investigation that had "thwarted terrorists."[62]

After the two convictions, a new prosecutor on the case produced two pieces of exculpatory evidence that had not been given to the defense. One of those was especially troubling, in that it called into question the reliability of the government's most important witness. The judge then ordered the government to formally review the case and to produce a report. In August 2004, the Justice Department issued the report, which seriously undermined the strength of its own case, even referring to it as a "three-legged stool." At that point, the Justice Department took the rather unusual step of moving to have the two defendants' convictions on the terrorism charges overturned.[63] In early September 2004, the judge threw out the terrorism-related convictions, noting that while prosecutors must be innovative in prosecuting terrorists, they must not act "outside the Constitution," which the judge said had occurred in this case. The judge also accused the prosecutors of having developed a theory on the case, and that they then "ignored or avoided any evidence or information which contradicted that view."[64]

The overturned terrorism conviction in Germany occurred in the case of Munir al-Motassadeq, an associate of Mzoudi and the "Hamburg cell" members. In August 2002, al-Motassadeq was charged with conspiracy to commit murder for his alleged role in the September 11 attacks, and also with being a member of a domestic terrorist organization. In all, he was charged with 3,066 counts of being an accessory to murder, based on the number of victims who died in the September 11 attacks.[65] The prosecutors contended that al-Motassadeq was a member of the group that planned the attacks, and that he helped provide logistical support for the hijackers while they were in the United States.[66] Al-Motassadeq denied advance knowledge or having played any role in September 11.[67] After a lengthy trial, al-Motassadeq was convicted by a panel of German judges and sentenced to fifteen years in prison. Soon after that conviction, Mzoudi was acquitted of almost identical charges. Al-Motassadeq appealed his conviction, stating that his right to a fair trial had been compromised because the court did not have access to the information provided by the BKA in Mzoudi's trial. The appeals court granted al-Motassadeq's appeal and overturned his conviction.[68]

While Britain has not had terrorism convictions overturned, the prosecution efforts in one case did bear notable similarities to the "sleeper cell" case in Detroit. A man known to the court as "Ashraf" was charged by the British government under the 2000 Terrorism Act with possessing various terrorist materials, including information on how to build a bomb. Ashraf was arrested in June 2003 and was being held at Belmarsh, the infamous prison where the Part IV detainees were imprisoned. During the trial, it became clear that there was no fingerprint evidence connecting the defendant to the relevant "terrorist" materials. Ashraf pleaded guilty to having a false passport, but was not convicted of the terrorism charges. In announcing the sentence for the passport offense, the judge was highly critical of the prosecution's efforts in the case. The judge argued that the case had a "bad history" and that the prosecution's strategy had "shifted and changed." The prosecution had also handled the trial exhibits poorly and failed to disclose evidence to the defense in a timely manner. Despite the problems in the case, the judge noted that the government had still treated Ashraf as a "category A" prisoner in Belmarsh. In the view of the judge, "This ought to be a matter of real concern to those who have overall charge of this prosecution." The judge asked prosecutors to relay his concerns to their superiors.[69]

No charges and dropped charges. While the United States, Germany, and Britain have all encountered serious trial obstacles in terrorism prosecutions, many other cases have never even made it to trial. All three countries have arrested individuals for suspected involvement in terrorist activity, but ultimately neglected to bring criminal charges against them.

Many examples of this have occurred in the United States. In one October 2001 incident that received considerable publicity, the FBI detained as material witnesses eight Egyptian nationals who were living in Evansville, Indiana. The arrests were based on what turned out to be a bogus tip. The FBI never filed criminal charges in the case, and in the end issued a public apology to the eight, asking a federal judge to expunge their arrest records.[70] In another highly publicized case, the FBI arrested Oregon lawyer Brandon Mayfield as a material witness in the Madrid train bombings. Spanish authorities had sent photographs of fingerprints found at the crime scene to law enforcement agencies throughout the world, including the FBI. The FBI believed that Mayfield's fingerprint matched the one in the photograph, and alerted Oregon authorities. Mayfield was released without charge when it turned out that the fingerprint was not, in fact, his.[71] Many others, in less publicized cases, have also been arrested by the U.S. government, only to be later released without charge.

In numerous cases in Britain and Germany, police have arrested individuals in the course of their counterterrorism investigations whom they subsequently released either without charge or after dropping the charges against them.[72] As discussed earlier, from September 11 to the end of 2004, British authorities arrested more than 700 people under the 2000 Terrorism Act powers. Almost half of these individuals were subsequently released without any charge.[73] For example, in March 2003, British police arrested eight men in Derbyshire under the 2000 Terrorism Act powers. They were arrested based on their connections to Omar Sharif, a British national who attempted to commit a suicide attack in Israel, but failed when his bomb did not explode. All eight were subsequently freed without charge.[74] In another case, three individuals were arrested under the Terrorism Act powers for their suspicious activity near the headquarters of GCHQ, a British national security agency. They, too, were later released without charge.[75] The history is similar in Germany.[76] For example, German authorities released one of the individuals detained for the alleged plot to assassinate interim Iraqi Prime Minister Iyad Allawi.[77]

While many of the individuals detained during counterterrorism investigations by the U.S., British, and German governments have been eventually released, the inability of the government to bring terrorism charges does not always lead to the suspects' release. Britain and Germany both employ versions of the U.S. "spitting on the sidewalk" approach, and often use any legal tools at their disposal to neutralize suspected terrorists. These tools include immigration powers and the use of nonterrorism-related criminal statutes.

Are failed prosecutions always an indication of innocence? As will be considered at length later, the mixed results and problems encountered by governments in terrorism prosecutions have led to a great deal of criticism from the media and general public. Some of this criticism is certainly fair, and innocent people have been caught up in aggressive law enforcement efforts. However, the fact that an individual is not convicted on terrorism charges should not necessarily be viewed in every case as a complete vindication. Although in many cases defendants have been found to be innocent of the charges against them, in other cases troubling information has persisted about individuals' ties to terrorism that the government was unable to prove in a criminal trial. In fact, there have been cases where the terrorism charges have failed, but where the judges have made clear that they remain deeply concerned about an individual's terrorism connections. In other cases, government officials have remarked that despite the failed terrorism charges, they are still suspicious that the individual is involved in terrorist-related activity.

In the "Virginia jihad" case, for example, the judge remarked after acquitting Benkhala of the terrorism charges that she did not consider it to be a complete vindication. The judge stated that while prosecutors had demonstrated that Benkhala was very interested in "violent jihad," they had not proved beyond a reasonable doubt that Benkhala actually traveled to Afghanistan and fought with the Taliban. The judge added that she was disturbed nonetheless by Benkhala's conduct, noting, "This business about violent jihad and it being part of what good Muslims view as part of their religion, I have to say it troubles this court greatly and I hope it troubles some of you."[78] In addition, in throwing out the terrorism charges against another one of the defendants before trial, the judge issued a somewhat cautionary note, stating that although the charges were being dismissed, the defendant did appear to believe in a "radical form of Islam."[79]

In several of the acquittals in Germany, judges made similar comments about the defendants at the end of the trial. In acquitting Ihsan Garnaoui of terrorism charges, the judge said that while prosecutors had failed to prove their case, the court was still convinced that Garnaoui supported violence and had come to Germany intending to commit at least "one attack with explosives."[80] The judge went on to say that Garnaoui did not "just have evil thoughts, but also wanted to transform those thoughts into action." The judge remarked that the court could not go further in its ruling, however, because the prosecutors did not prove that Garnaoui was a recruiter for a terrorist organization, noting, "General discussions about the question of whether one may take violent action against 'nonbelievers' does not constitute (attempted) creation of a terrorist group."[81] The judge in the Mzoudi trial also made clear, upon finding Mzoudi not guilty of terrorism charges, that the court was not persuaded of his innocence, but rather that he was being acquitted merely because of the lack of evidence.[82] Finally, in the trial of Boudid-Abdelkader O, the judge acquitted him on terrorism charges but denied him compensation for the period he spent in prison prior to the trial. The judge defended this decision by noting that defendant had been "grossly negligent" in drawing suspicion to himself by attending a training camp in Afghanistan and by associating with the other defendants in the case.[83]

A judge in Britain made a similar remark at the conclusion of a failed terrorism prosecution, questioning the innocence of the defendants. In this case, four individuals with connections to the "ricin" poison-recipes case were originally charged with terrorism- and chemical-weapons-related offenses. The prosecution ultimately dropped the terrorism and chemical weapons charges against two of the defendants, leaving only the offense of possessing false passports. The defendants pleaded guilty to that count. Despite the fact that the more serious charges were dropped, the judge in the case clearly still considered the two to be quite dangerous, recommending that they be deported after serving their prison time because he believed that they were "a detriment to this country."[84]

In a number of other unsuccessful terrorism prosecutions, it was not the judge but government officials who indicated their continued concern about the defendants' terrorism connections. While comments from government officials with a stake in the outcome carry less weight than those made by independent judges, they are still worth noting. In the U.S. government's case against Arnaout, for example, after Arnaout pleaded guilty to a nonterrorism felony charge, his attorney stated that his client had been cleared of ties to terrorism. United States Attorney Patrick Fitzgerald contested the attorney's characterization, saying, "We were prepared to prove and still are prepared to prove" that BIF was working with al-Qaeda.[85] Other senior law enforcement officials agreed with Fitzgerald, and still believed that BIF had "substantial and very troubling links" to al-Qaeda and the international jihadist movement. In their view, the leadership of the organization endorsed, and in some cases supported, extremist and jihadist ideology. Senior FBI agents conceded, however, that many in the Islamic community in Chicago viewed the end result—with Arnaout pleading guilty to a nonterrorism-related felony charge—as a vindication. These agents agreed that many in these communities saw the government as having unjustly targeted Arnaout.[86]

In Britain, at the conclusion of the case against the eight individuals ulti-mately cleared of charges related to their involvement in the alleged "poison plot," government officials indicated that their suspicions were not entirely alleviated by the outcome of the prosecution. The British Home Secretary stated, in reference to the eight defendants, "We will obviously keep a very close eye on the eight men being freed today, and consider exactly what to do in the light of this decision."[87] German officials expressed similar sen-timents after Ihsan Garnaoui was acquitted on terrorism charges. Rainer Wendt, vice president of the German Police Union, stated that the verdict was "completely incomprehensible to the police, and dangerous in its effect," claiming that the evidence provided should have been adequate for a convic-tion.[88] German government officials were also distressed with the Mzoudi acquittal, remarking that the court was not "well advised" and that the judge should have "slept on the decision for the night."[89] The German government subsequently denied Mzoudi's visa request to stay in the country, presum-ably regarding Mzoudi as dangerous despite his acquittal.[90]

Notes

1. Justice Department, "Report from the Field: The USA PATRIOT Act at Work," July 2004.

2. "Ashcroft Details Uses of Patriot Act," Associated Press, July 13, 2004.

3. Justice Department, "Report from the Field"; David Cole, "Taking Liberties—Ashcroft: 0 for 5,000," Nation, October 4, 2004; Andrew McCarthy, "Winning and Losing," National Review Online, June 21, 2004. The Justice Department argues for its successes, while Cole argues that with the overturning of the Detroit verdict, Ashcroft was 0 for 5,000 in his post–September 11 terrorism efforts (5,000 is the number of people Cole wrote the department had detained since September 11). Others have made similar statements. New York Times columnist Paul Krugman assessed Ashcroft as the "worst attorney general in history," stating that there had been no major successful post–September 11 prosecutions.

4. These reports will be discussed at greater length later in the monograph.

5. Dan Eggen and Julie Tate, "U.S. Campaign Produces Few Convictions on Terrorism Charges: Statistics Often Count Lesser Crimes," Washington Post, June 12, 2005. Eggen and Tate reach a similar conclusion based on their comprehensive review of the post–September 11 prosecutions in the United States.

6. Craig Whitlock, "Terror Suspects Beating Charges Filed in Europe," Washington Post, May 31, 2004. Britain and Germany are hardly alone among European countries in

having difficulty prosecuting terrorist suspects since September 11. For example, in Italy, nine Moroccans were acquitted of plotting to poison the U.S. embassy's water supply; twenty-eight Pakistanis were cleared of charges that they were conspiring with both al-Qaeda and the Italian mafia to kill a British admiral; and three Egyptians were unsuccessfully charged with plotting to blow up an American military cemetery and the airport in Rome.

7. Scotland Yard official, interview by author, January 2005. British counterterrorism experts argue that the statistics are not an effective way of judging the success of their counterterrorism efforts. They note that cases are very slow to proceed through the system, and so there will probably be many additional convictions in the future. They also state that a number of those arrested for counterterrorism offenses were eventually prosecuted successfully under nonterrorism-related offenses.

8. Jerry Markon, "Muslim Leader Is Found Guilty, Fairfax Man Urged Followers to Train for Violent Jihad," *Washington Post*, April 27, 2005.

9. "Yemeni Cleric, Assistant Convicted of Terror-Funding Charges," CNN, March 10, 2005.

10. Julia Preston, "Civil Rights Lawyer Is Convicted of Aiding Terrorists," *New York Times*, February 10, 2005.

11. Jerry Markon, "Final Defendant in 'Va. Jihad' Case Acquitted," *Washington Post*, September 3, 2004.

12. "Defendants Convicted in Northern Virginia 'Jihad' Trial," Department of Justice press release, March 4, 2004.

13. "Shoe Bomber Gets Life in Prison," CBS News, January 30, 2003 (available online at www.cbsnews.com/stories/2003/01/31/attack/main538727.shtml); John Pistole (Executive Assistant Director, FBI Counterterrorism/Counterintelligence), in statement before the 9-11 Commission, April 14, 2004; "Iyman Faris Sentenced for Providing Material Support to al-Qaeda," Justice Department press release, October 28, 2003.

14. Duncan Campbell, "Police Killer Gets 17 Years for Poison Plot," *Guardian* (London), April 14, 2005.

15. Jill Lawless, "Eight of Nine Suspects Cleared of London Ricin Plot," Associated Press, April 13, 2005; Michael Holden and Peter Graff, "Algerian Convicted in Ricin Strike Plot," Reuters, April 13, 2005.

16. Holden and Graff, "Algerian Convicted."

17. "Mystery Still Surrounds Killer," BBC News, April 13, 2005. Available online (http://newswww.bbc.net.uk/1/hi/uk/4440953.stm).

18. Campbell, "Police Killer Gets 17."

19. John Steele, "Nine Years for Jihad Message of Death: Muslim Cleric Will Be Deported after Serving Prison Term for Soliciting Murder and Stirring Up Racial Hatred," *Daily Telegraph* (London), March 8, 2003; "London Muslim Cleric Sentenced for Soliciting Murder," *Jerusalem Post*, February 25, 2003.

20. As will be discussed at greater length later in the study, pleas are rare in British cases because Britain does not have U.S.-style plea bargaining. Badat therefore had to plead guilty without knowing whether or not the plea would benefit him in the sentencing phase of the trial. Britain has considered making changes to move toward the United States in this area.

21. Jason Bennetto, "British Muslim Admits Plot to Blow Up Airliner," *Independent* (London), March 1, 2005.

22. "Terrorist Sentenced to Four Years," *Deutsche Welle*, November 26, 2003. Available online (www.dw-world/de/dw/article/0,,1041971,00.html).

23. "Four Convicted in Strasbourg Terror Plot," *Deutsche Welle*, March 11, 2003. Available online (www.dw-world.de/dw/article/0,,802558,00.html).

24. Steve Bird, "Immigrants Who Funded al-Qaeda Jailed for 11 Years," *Times* (London), April 2, 2003.

25. Bird, "Immigrants Who Funded al-Qaeda."

26. Jerry Markon, "Case Dismissed against Alleged Jihad Group Member," *Washington Post*, February 21, 2004.

27. See "Defendants Convicted in Northern Virginia."

28. 9-11 Commission, *Final Report*, p. 273.

29. "Indictment of Zacarias Moussaoui," December 2001 (*U.S. v. Moussaoui*, Eastern District of Virginia).

30. Robert Mueller (FBI director), in statement at Department of Justice press conference announcing the indictment of Zacarias Moussaoui, December 11, 2001.

31. Neil A. Lewis, "Moussaoui's Guilty Plea Leaves Unresolved Issues," *New York Times*, April 24, 2005; Indictment of Zacarias Moussaoui.

32. "Saudi National Charged with Conspiracy to Provide Material Support to Hamas and Other Violent Jihadists," Department of Justice press release, March 4, 2004.

33. Maureen O'Hagan, "A Terrorism Case That Went Awry," *Seattle Times*, November 22, 2004; available online (http://seattletimes.nwsource.com/html/localnews/2002097570_sami22m.html). The governor of Idaho made similar comments. At a press conference, after the initial arrest in early 2003, the governor said that the arrest vindicated his previously "vague references" to the terrorist threat in Idaho. It should be noted that

Ashcroft announced this indictment at a press conference where he was also announcing developments in three other terrorist-related cases. His broad statements cited were intended to cover all the cases, not just the al-Hussayen case.

34. O'Hagan, "A Terrorism Case That Went Awry."

35. "U.S. Government Case against Saudi Suspect Questioned by Judge," Agence France Presse, April 30, 2004.

36. O'Hagan, "A Terrorism Case That Went Awry."

37. "The Verdicts," *Detroit Free Press*, June 4, 2003.

38. David Runk, "Jury Convicts 2 Arab Immigrants, Acquits 2 of Conspiring to Support Terrorism," Associated Press, June 3, 2003.

39. Markon, "Final Defendant."

40. Markon, "Case Dismissed."

41. "Two Albany Mosque Leaders Indicted on 19 Counts," Associated Press, August 10, 2004. Available online (www.usatoday.com/news/nation/2004-08/10-albany-arrests_x.htm).

42. Ellen Wulfhorst, "U.S. Judge Blasts FBI Case against Albany Muslims," Reuters, August 24, 2004.

43. Jill Lawless, "Eight of Nine Suspects Cleared of London Ricin Plot," Associated Press, April 13, 2005.

44. Michael Holden and Peter Graff, "Algerian Convicted in Ricin Strike Plot," Reuters, April 13, 2005. The case was particularly damaging for Britain because of the amount of publicity and press attention it received. Initially, the media reported that the police had found actual poison during the raid, and the press and public began referring to the case as the "ricin case." When it turned out that only poison recipes and no actual poison had been found, the government was accused by the media and the public of overhyping the case. The government's failure to convict eight of the nine defendants only increased the criticism directed at the government.

45. "Suicide Bomber Wife Cleared," BBC News, July 8, 2004. Available online (http://news.bbc.co.uk/1/hi/uk/3876759.stm).

46. Gethin Chamberlain, "Chef Cleared of Web Site Terror Plot," *Scotsman*, August 10, 2002.

47. "Moroccan Student Charged in 9/11 Case," Agence France Presse, May 9, 2003. Available online (http://iafrica.com/news/worldnews/235291.htm).

48. John Burgess, "Court Frees Moroccan Convicted in 9/11 Case," *Washington Post*, April 8, 2004.

49. Loammi Blaauw-Wolf, "The Hamburg Terror Trials—American Political Poker and German Legal Procedure: An Unlikely Combination to Fight International Terrorism," *German Law Journal* 5, no. 7 (July 2004). Available online (www.germanlawjournal. com/article.php?id=473).

50. "German Court Acquits Algerian Defendant of Terror Charges," BBC Monitoring International Reports, December 12, 2003.

51. 9-11 Commission, *Staff Monograph on Terrorist Financing*.

52. In January of 2002, BIF filed a civil suit against the federal government contesting the government's actions, and saying that its activities were lawful. In April 2002, Arnaout and BIF were charged with two counts of perjury, based on a declaration that Arnaout filed in the civil suit. When this charge against Arnaout was dismissed, the government filed an obstruction of justice charge against him.

53. John Ashcroft, in prepared remarks at press conference, October 9, 2002. Available online (www.usdoj.gov/ag/speeches/2002/100902agremarksbifindictment.htm).

54. 9-11 Commission, *Staff Monograph on Terrorist Financing*, p. 109.

55. Matt Surman, "Germany Acquits Suspect of Terror Charges," Associated Press, April 6, 2005.

56. Mark Trevelyan, "Two Failed Terrorism Trials Raise Worry in Europe," Reuters, April 8, 2005.

57. Craig Whitlock, "Terror Suspects Beating Charges Filed in Europe," *Washington Post*, May 31, 2004.

58. Surman, "Germany Acquits."

59. "Criminal Complaint," September 18, 2001 (*U.S. v. Karim Koubriti*); "Second Superceding Indictment," August 28, 2002 (*U.S. v. Koubriti*).

60. Danny Hakim and Eric Lichtblau, "After Convictions, the Undoing of a U.S. Terror Prosecution," *New York Times*, October 7, 2004. Ashcroft's claim violated a gag order that had been imposed by the judge, and these statements were retracted by the Justice Department within several days.

61. Edward Spannaus, "Scare Tactics: Ashcroft's Phony 'War on Terrorism,'" *Executive Intelligence Review*, March 26, 2004. In response, the judge stated he was "distressed to see the Attorney General commenting in the middle of a trial about the credibility of a witness who had just gotten off the stand."

62. Hakim and Lichtblau, "After Convictions."

63. Ibid.

64. Danny Hakim, "Judge Reverses Convictions in Detroit Terrorism Case," *New York Times*, September 3, 2004.

65. At the time, as was discussed earlier, it was not illegal to be a member of a foreign terrorist organization. Therefore, to convict Motassadeq, the Germans had to prove that he was a member of a domestic terrorist organization.

66. "Man Charged over Sept 11 Involvement," *Guardian* (London), August 29, 2002; 9-11 Commission, *Final Report*, p. 167. The 9-11 Commission found that Motassadeq did take actions to help conceal the travel of the "Hamburg cell" members to Afghanistan.

67. Richard Bernstein, "Germans Free Moroccan Convicted of a 9/11 Role," *New York Times*, April 8, 2004.

68. Ibid.

69. "Judge Hits Out after Accused Walks Free," *Birmingham* Post, March 24, 2004.

70. Kim Barker and Matt O'Connor, "9/11 Detainees Win U.S. Apology, Clean Record," *Chicago Tribune*, June 12, 2003; Michael Moss, "False Terrorism Tips to FBI Uproot the Lives of Suspects," *New York Times*, June 19, 2003. Four of the individuals' names were then put into a national criminal database as suspected terrorists, which then made it difficult—if not impossible—for them to find jobs, places to live, and to fly.

71. David Stout, "Report Faults FBI's Fingerprint Scrutiny in Arrest of Lawyer," *New York Times*, November 17, 2004.

72. Audrey Gillan, "Home Office Says Sorry to Suspects for Ricin Blunder," *Guardian* (London), April 16, 2005. Britain did apparently make an embarrassing mistake in the terrorism context. In an emergency request that ten individuals be subjected to "control orders," the British cited the individuals' connection to the "network of North African extremists directly involved in terrorist planning in the UK, including the use of toxic chemicals." Britain later conceded that the individuals were not connected to this alleged plot and that this information was included in the request because of a "clerical error." The Home Office maintained that although this information was inaccurate, the overall basis for the control order was still valid.

73. British Home Office, Terrorism Act 2000, Arrest and Charge Statistics. Available online (www.homeoffice.gov.uk/docs3/tatc_arrest_stats.html).

74. David Bamber, Daniel Foggo, et al., "MI5 Admits: We Let Suicide Bombers Slip through Net," *Sunday Telegraph* (London), May 4, 2003.

75. Helen Morgan, "Spy Centre Arrests: Trio Released," Press Association, January 20, 2003.

76. Francis Miko and Christian Froehlich, *Germany's Role in Fighting Terrorism: Implications for U.S. Policy* (Congressional Research Service, December 27, 2004), p. 8.

77. "German Police Release One of Four Men Held on Suspicion of Planning Attack on Iraqi Prime Minister," Associated Press, December 5, 2004.

78. Markon, "Final Defendant."

79. Markon, "Case Dismissed."

80. Surman, "Germany Acquits." See also "Germany to Appeal against Verdict in Tunisian Extremist Case," Agence France Presse, April 8, 2005.

81. Matt Surman, "Al Qaida Suspect Acquitted of Terrorism Charges, Jailed for Weapons, Tax Offenses, in Setback for German Prosecutors," Associated Press, April 6, 2005.

82. "Acquitted September 11 Suspect Denied German Study Visa," Agence France Presse, January 24, 2005.

83. "German Court Acquits."

84. Shenai Raif, "Brothers Jailed for Holding False Passports," Press Association, June 12, 2003.

85. Matthew Epstein, "Terrorism Trial Ends with a Whimper," *National Review Online*, February 11, 2003.

86. 9-11 Commission, *Terrorist Financing Monograph*, pp. 110–111.

87. Duncan Campbell, Vikram Dodd, et al., "Police Killer Gets 17 Years for Poison Plot," *Guardian* (London), April 14, 2005.

88. Trevelyan, "Two Failed."

89. "Mzoudi Decision Generates Criticism and Skepticism," *Deutsche World*, December 12, 2003. Available online (www.dw-world.de/dw/article/0,,1058508,00.html).

90. See "Acquitted September 11 Suspect."

Obstacles to Successful Terrorism Prosecution

AWIDE VARIETY OF FACTORS HAVE CONTRIBUTED to the problems in terrorism prosecutions in the United States and Europe. What is notable is the extent to which these factors have been similar. Chief among the difficulties is the great deal of pressure to disrupt terrorist cells much earlier than would have been the case before September 11. No longer do governments have the luxury of waiting until just before a possible attack to make arrests, with the expectation of catching the perpetrators "red-handed." As discussed earlier, the scale of the September 11 attacks and the recognition of the potential lethality of future attacks has dictated a change in strategy: when thousands or more could perish in a single attack, the calculus for both policymakers and law enforcement officials changes. "The risk of waiting is just too great now," says the U.S. attorney in Houston. "Once we see that a threat is plausible, that it's real, and that a person has the intent to carry it out and takes some steps to show it's not just idle talk, that's enough for us to move."[1]

Dale Watson, the former chief of terrorism at the FBI, explained the dilemma facing U.S. policymakers: "There are no guarantees in this business...[I]f you're the president or if you're the vice president...and somebody tells you...'Well, there's a real high probability they're not going to do anything, and we want to watch them for a while,' they'll say, 'Hmmmm. I don't think so.'"[2] French interior minister Nicolas Sarkozy expressed similar sentiments in explaining why French officials pressed for immediate law enforcement action in a case involving a possible chemical attack in Europe. "When you are dealing with suspects like this," said Sarkozy, "it is better to arrest them before, not after."[3] Consequently, governments are often left prosecuting individuals whom they believe were involved in terrorist activity, but about whom the government either does not know the exact details, or where the details are too difficult to prove.

Selected cases in both Europe and the United States illustrate the difficulty of achieving the right balance, and why the earlier law enforcement intervention often makes for more difficult prosecutions. The Garnaoui prosecution in Germany, for example, was plagued by problems, with prosecutors unable to establish even basic details of the planned attacks, including such facts as the targets and the intended participants.[4] Moreover, the German government was forced to concede in court that two of the primary confidential informants in the case did not even know Garnaoui, but received the relevant information from third parties. In fact, after several months of trial, the judge suggested that the prosecutors drop the terrorism-related charges and attempt to proceed on other charges (specifically, tax evasion and forgery).[5] After Garnaoui was acquitted of the terrorism charges, the prosecutors conceded that the strength of their case might have been hurt by the early intervention of German law enforcement officials. In closing arguments, one prosecutor emphasized this point by noting, "We cannot wait until attacks have been carried out and the dead are lying on the street."[6]

In one British case, initial reports indicated that the government had possibly prevented a potentially catastrophic poison gas attack on the Underground subway by arresting and charging three North African men on terrorism charges. However, none of the three were ultimately convicted of the terrorism charges.[7] While government sources stated that separate intelligence indicated a "clear intention" by the men to attack the London subway (a revelation that may have increased the hysteria surrounding the arrests), there was ultimately no evidence that the three were involved in planning such an attack. The government subsequently acknowledged that the men had been arrested as part of the government's new strategy to disrupt terrorist cells at "an early stage."[8]

In another case in Britain, police received information from the intelligence services about a possible upcoming attack outside London. Though the threat did not appear to be imminent, police elected not to wait and gather additional information to build a stronger case; instead they made a precautionary arrest. The government did not have enough evidence at the time to bring terrorism charges, and ended up bringing unrelated criminal charges instead.[9] Of course, there's no certainty that the government would have unearthed an actual plot had it waited longer in any of these cases. Nevertheless, these examples do illustrate the difficult situation—and the information vacuum—that governments frequently face with a strategy of earlier intervention.

The U.S. case involving the so-called "Lackawanna Six" demonstrates the increased difficulty in catching defendants red-handed after September 11. In September 2002, six American citizens of Yemeni descent were arrested and charged with providing, and conspiring to provide, material support and resources to a foreign terrorist organization. The criminal complaint also listed three unindicted coconspirators. The government alleged in the complaint that the defendants had attended the al-Farooq terrorist training camp in Afghanistan in the spring and summer of 2001, where they received military training and had the opportunity to hear Osama bin Laden deliver a speech.[10] During the speech, bin Laden espoused "anti-American and anti-Israel statements" and discussed how important it was to "train and fight for the cause of Islam." He also discussed an upcoming fight against the Americans.[11] In the bail hearing, the government argued that the men should be denied bail because they posed a danger to the community and were also a flight risk. To make this argument, the prosecutors referred to a cryptic e-mail one of the individuals had sent telling of a "big meal" that no one would be able to withstand "except for those with faith."[12] Ultimately, all six pleaded guilty to supporting terrorism and are serving sentences of between seven and ten years in prison.[13] While the government has repeatedly referred to this case as an example of a successful disruption of a terrorist cell, government officials have conceded that they do not know exactly what the six men were planning. The head of the FBI's office in Buffalo stated, after the six were arrested, "We did not find, at this point, anything specific that they were planning." At the conclusion of the case, the U.S. attorney expressed similar sentiments: "We may never know what, if anything, was planned. But to the extent that we brought them this far, something may have been prevented."[14]

Senior FBI officials explained their difficulty in deciding how to handle a case like this in the post–September 11 world. FBI director Robert Mueller stated, "Do . . . the American people want us to take [a] chance, if we have information where we believe that a group of individuals is poised to commit a terrorist act in the United States that'll kill Americans? [Should we just] let it go and wait for the attack, and then after the fact conduct our investigation? I think not." Dale Watson, then the FBI's head of terrorism, posed the dilemma facing the bureau: "Can you guarantee they're not going to do anything?" The answer, of course, is no, and in the Lackawanna case a conscious decision was made, according to Watson, to "get them out of here." Director Mueller acknowledged differences of opinion in the government about the facts in this case but noted there would be "differences of opinion in just about every intelligence analysis you make."[15]

For the United States, the material support statute has been the key tool enabling the government to employ a strategy of earlier intervention. According to Christopher Wray, former head of the Justice Department's criminal division, "The material support statutes enable us to strike earlier and earlier." Wray noted, "We would much rather catch a terrorist with his hands on a check than on a bomb."[16] According to the Justice Department, as of May 2004 more than fifty defendants in seventeen different judicial districts had been charged under the statute since September 11. These include John Walker Lindh, the so-called "American Taliban"; the six Yemenis in Lackawanna who attended an al-Qaeda training camp; an Ohio truck driver who scouted various U.S. sites on al-Qaeda's behalf; the Saudi student in Idaho who served as the administrator for a website allegedly containing jihadist material; and some of the paintball players in Virginia who were charged with providing support to a Kashmiri terrorist group. In assessing the statute, a senior FBI official testified before Congress, "It would be difficult to overstate the importance of the material support statutes to our ongoing counterterrorism efforts.[17]

The types of cases being brought under the strategy of early intervention in the United States can be contrasted with terrorism prosecutions before September 11. In the earlier terrorism cases, when prosecutions often took place after an attack—or at least much further into the planning stages—defendants were charged with offenses relating to actual terrorist plots, and not with "material support."[18] In comparing U.S. cases before and after September 11, Andy McCarthy, a former federal prosecutor in New York, noted that from 1993 to 2001, the U.S. government had a 100 percent success rate in prosecuting terrorism-related cases; every defendant who went to trial on terrorism-related charges was eventually convicted. McCarthy said that this was not attributable to better training or better lawyering by the prosecutors, but rather to the fact that before September 11, they had "much better cases." The early high-profile terrorism prosecutions were either for terrorist actions that had already occurred, such as the first World Trade Center attack or the U.S. embassy bombings, or for plots that had been fully formed, like Ramzi Yousef's plan to blow up twelve airplanes. In McCarthy's view, "If the government adheres to the comprehensive post-9/11 approach that seeks to eradicate rather than manage the terrorist threat, prosecutors will rarely, if ever, have such juicy cases again."[19]

While McCarthy was commenting on the cases being brought in the United States, his analysis is also relevant for the Europeans. As one European counterterrorism expert noted, in commenting on some of the failed terrorism prosecutions in Europe, "If I make a plan in my study at home to blow up the U.S. embassy, and if those plans are discovered, that will never be enough to send me to prison for a terrorist plot. The actual execution has to have started. That's very complicated and depends very much on the opinion of the judges." [20] However, because they realize that terrorist acts are potentially so catastrophic, government officials in Europe and the United States are not willing to improve their odds of a conviction by waiting until the plot has progressed.

The second reason successful prosecution of suspected terrorists has become so difficult is that it is often problematic to use intelligence information in the course of a prosecution.[21] This is a two-pronged issue involving both the admissibility of intelligence information, and the often very difficult balancing question of protecting sources and methods.

The issue of admissibility is more of a problem under the U.S. and British systems than for the Germans and other continental European countries with civil law systems. In fact, according to an experienced British barrister, the primary reason terrorism prosecutions fail in Britain is related to the rules of evidence, and resulting evidential difficulties.[22] Both Britain and the United States have strict rules governing what information can be admitted into the trial record. Information that does not meet the reliability standards, is unfairly prejudicial, or cannot be proven to a reasonable degree is not admissible in U.S. or British trials. Germany, like other continental European countries, does not have to rely only on "direct" evidence. The judges have far more latitude to admit and consider information in the course of their deliberations, information that would be excluded under U.S. and British law. For example, German judges can admit information that would be considered "hearsay" under British and U.S. law. The continental systems allow judges to use their discretion and experience in determining how to assess this information. The German standard of proof instructs the judge to decide "on the result of the evidence taken according to its free conviction gained from the hearing as a whole." If the judge determines that the information is not credible, he does not have to give it any weight in the decision.[23]

In the United States and Britain, the hearsay rules often pose the greatest challenges to criminal proceedings.[24] As former federal prosecutor Paul Rosenzweig points out, the best information for the government is often "rankest hearsay." Rosenzweig's illustrative example of such information is this: "At a meeting last week, Osama said ...," a statement that would obviously be incredibly valuable intelligence, but would be inadmissible in a criminal proceeding.[25] There have been a number of occasions since September 11 in which U.S. and British judges have ruled potentially valuable information as inadmissible. For example, in the "ricin" case in Britain, the initial tip about Bourgass and his associates came from an Algerian named Muhammad Meguerba. After providing the tip to British police, Meguerba fled back to Algeria. During subsequent interrogations by the Algerian security services, Meguerba provided a great deal of information that would have helped the prosecution's case. Meguerba apparently acknowledged that he and Bourgass had spent time in Afghanistan, and together devised a poison plot that they planned to carry out in London. Meguerba also stated that their cell was led by two al-Qaeda figures. The judge ruled, however, that Meguerba's statements in Algeria were inadmissible, since he was not available for cross-examination.[26]

In the Arnaout case in the United States, the prosecution's case was seriously hurt by a judge's ruling excluding as "hearsay" information that tied Arnaout to al-Qaeda.[27] The prosecutors argued that the material was admissible under one of the hearsay exceptions, which allowed for this type of information in conspiracy cases, but the judge found that the prosecutors had failed to prove the existence of a conspiracy.[28] A week after the judge's ruling, the government and Arnaout reached a plea agreement on the nonterrorism-related felony charge.[29] In the case against Yemeni Sheikh al-Moayad, the prosecutors suffered an equally damaging ruling, but Moayad was ultimately convicted nonetheless. In that case, the judge ruled before trial that the prosecutors could not present information that they argued tied Moayad to suspected al-Qaeda members in Afghanistan and Croatia. The prosecution planned to introduce address books seized from suspected al-Qaeda members in the former Yugoslavia, in which Moayad's name and contact information were listed. The prosecution also hoped to place in evidence an admission form from an al-Qaeda training camp, in which Moayad was listed as a reference. The judge excluded all of this information, finding the address books too "remote" to be relevant, and the admission form not on its own evidence of guilt—without knowing whose form it was.[30]

There is an even more difficult issue than admissibility, however, regarding the use of intelligence in criminal proceedings. Governments have to determine whether it is worth disclosing the intelligence source or its method of discovery, to increase their odds in prosecutions.[31] Both Britain and the United States have adversarial systems, under which accused individuals have the right to challenge all evidence against them. The evidence must be produced in the presence of the defendant at a public hearing, which means the defense has the right to see all potentially relevant material, even if the prosecutor is not relying on it. While both the U.S. and British systems permit judges to withhold from the defendant relevant information—under the Classified Information Procedures Act (CIPA) in the United States, and the Public Interest Immunity law (PII) in Britain—these are hardly perfect solutions.[32] There are occasions when the judge may rule against the government and decide that the information must be admitted regardless of its sensitivity. There are also cases where the government may determine that though the information is sensitive, without it, the case will be seriously impaired. For example, during the embassy bombing trial, the U.S. government made the decision to introduce an al-Qaeda training manual into evidence.[33] Within days, media articles broadcast this development—and more worryingly, summaries of the manual—throughout the world.[34] The primary concern here, of course, is the disclosure to terrorist organizations of information the U.S. government has collected about them.

During the course of terrorism prosecutions, valuable information can also be unintentionally disclosed by the prosecuting authority. For example, according to the 9-11 Commission, the prosecutions in the 1990s of Islamic terrorists had the "unintended consequence of alerting some al-Qaeda members to the U.S. government's interest in them." In early 1995, for example, the government listed in a confidential court document Osama bin Laden and a number of other individuals as potential coconspirators in the so-called "New York City Landmarks" case. One of the individuals on the list obtained a copy and faxed it to one bin Laden's aides for distribution.[35] Dan Benjamin and Steve Simon, two Clinton-era National Security Council officials, provide in the preface to their book *The Age of Sacred Terror* an even better illustration of how much valuable information is made publicly available in the course of terrorism trials. Simon and Benjamin note that a great deal of information in the book was derived from transcripts of the terrorism trials before September 11. In the authors' view, the 50,000 pages of available transcripts in the case were a "treasure trove" that yielded far more about al-Qaeda than they had expected. In fact, they wondered why some of the information had not been brought to their attention while they were working at the National Security Council.[36]

German prosecutors do not face the same legal hurdles in terms of the admissibility of intelligence into trials, though they too have difficulties associated with using intelligence material in criminal proceedings. In particular, the German government must still decide whether it is worth disclosing information that might reveal sources or methods. In the Garnaoui case, for example, the prosecution's case was based largely on statements by two unidentified informants. The police would not allow them to testify in the trial, out of concern about disclosing their identity, though the judges were free to consider the informants' statements as part of the trial record. The refusal to allow the informants' testimony appears to have had a detrimental impact on the prosecution's case. In its opinion acquitting Garnaoui of the terrorism charges, the court stated that it found the informants' statements unreliable, as they were contradictory and often included hearsay.[37] A similar issue hurt the prosecutions' cases in the Mzoudi and Motassadeq trials. As discussed previously, toward the end of the Mzoudi trial—after Motassadeq had already been convicted—the court received a fax from the BKA that provided potentially exculpatory information about Mzoudi. The BKA either could not or would not supply any additional information about the identity of the "unidentified informer" who had exonerated Mzoudi, which ultimately resulted in his acquittal and the overturning of Mottasadeq's conviction.

In many cases in the United States and Britain, the difficulties in using intelligence in criminal prosecutions have been compounded because both the admissibility issues and the concern about sources and methods are at play. In fact, both of these factors were at the heart of the decision by the British government to establish the Special Immigration Appeals Commission process, which allowed it to indefinitely detain without a criminal trial non-British citizens suspected of terrorism.[38] This part of the act was designed for situations where the government believed that both prosecution and deportation were impossible, because the relevant information they had acquired was either inadmissible or too sensitive to disclose. As Lord Rooker stated in the House of Lords debate, "Detention under Part 4 will only be used for a limited number of people, where no other response is possible. If we consider that there is sufficient admissible evidence to bring a prosecution, we will seek to do so at any point in the process. If we can prosecute, we will."[39]

In the United States, the Jose Padilla and Moussaoui cases both provide a valuable illustration of how concerns about the admissibility of intelligence information, as well as the desire to protect intelligence sources and methods, can make daunting the prospect of a criminal trial. The FBI arrested Padilla, a U.S. citizen, in May 2002 at O'Hare Airport in Chicago, under a material witness warrant. In June of that year, he was declared an enemy combatant by President Bush and transferred to the custody of the Defense Department.[40] The information against Padilla, according to the Justice Department, came from Padilla's own statements, "from the statements of other al-Qaeda detainees, and from intelligence sources around the world." According to the department, Padilla admitted to having attended an al-Qaeda training camp in Afghanistan, an admission corroborated by the fact that the FBI had actually located his application to the camp. Padilla also conceded that he had been asked by Mohammed Atef, then bin Laden's deputy, whether he would be willing to blow up apartment buildings in the United States. After agreeing to do so, Padilla was then trained by an al-Qaeda explosives expert. Padilla said that he and an associate later approached Abu Zubaida and proposed an operation that involved detonating an improvised nuclear bomb in the United States. Zubaida, however, was skeptical and told them to try a dirty bomb instead.[41]

Though the information described by the Justice Department sounds rather damning, it would have been a very difficult—if not impossible—case to prosecute. The department stated that it could not have prosecuted Padilla without jeopardizing intelligence sources. In addition, the Justice Department officials noted that much of the information came from Padilla himself while he was in Defense Department custody, and that this information couldn't be used in a criminal trial. Had Padilla an attorney, in the Justice Department's view, he would have likely followed his lawyer's advice and said nothing. The Justice Department asserted that had it tried to charge Padilla, he would likely have ended up a free man.[42] Many of these same difficulties were also at play in the Moussaoui case. Before his guilty plea, Moussaoui managed to tie the legal system in knots. The most time-consuming and difficult issue raised by Moussaoui involved his requests for access to captured al-Qaeda members. This issue is at the heart of the difficulties in prosecuting suspected terrorists; it raises important constitutional questions regarding both a defendant's right to a fair trial and the government's ability to wage a war on terror effectively. Balancing these two interests is a difficult challenge, as has become clear during the Moussaoui case.

Some background on how this issue played out through the course of the Moussaoui litigation will help illustrate the difficulty of using sensitive intelligence in the course of general criminal prosecutions. More broadly, it demonstrates why this limitation makes prosecuting suspected terrorists infinitely more difficult. In the early stages of the proceedings, Moussaoui sought access to "Witness A," a captured member of al-Qaeda. The government refused access, but the district court concluded that this witness could offer "material testimony" to Moussaoui's defense. Though the judge acknowledged that this witness was a national security asset, she ruled that Moussaoui's right to a fair trial trumped the government's interest in secrecy. Moussaoui would be allowed to depose this witness by remote video. The government appealed the ruling, but the appeal was rejected on technical grounds. The government then offered a "substitution"—an alternative mechanism for Moussaoui to obtain this information—but the court rejected that as also inadequate. In the end, the government informed the court that, despite the earlier ruling, it would not grant access to this witness. Shortly thereafter, the court granted Moussaoui access to Witnesses "B" and "C" under the same conditions. The judge also subsequently rejected the government's proposed substitutions for Witnesses "B" and "C."[43]

In response to the government's refusal to provide Moussaoui access to these witnesses, the judge prohibited the prosecution from making any argument or offering any evidence of Moussaoui's involvement in the September 11 attacks, and dismissed the possibility of sentencing him to death. The government appealed the district court's rulings to the United States Court of Appeals for the Fourth Circuit. In September 2004, the appeals court upheld the district court's ruling that Moussaoui should have access to these witnesses and that the government's proposed substitutions were inadequate. The appeal courts reversed the district court, however, in its finding that it was not possible to craft adequate substitutions. Sending the case back to the district court, the appeals court instructed the judge to work with the parties to devise appropriate substitutions. The appeals court also restored the possibility of the death penalty and permitted the government to once again present evidence related to the September 11 attacks.[44] Moussaoui appealed the Fourth Circuit's ruling to the Supreme Court.[45]

The fact that Moussaoui was able to tie the system in knots was particularly striking in light of his behavior during the course of the proceedings. Moussaoui made a variety of statements—both in court and in written pleadings—attacking the U.S. government and acknowledging his extremist leanings. For example, in an August 2002 hearing, Moussaoui informed the judge that he wished to fire his court-appointed lawyers and represent himself. Moussaoui went on to say that he prayed to Allah for the "destruction of the United States of America," and for the "destruction of the Jewish people and state." Moussaoui stated that he was ready to fight and he accepted the government's characterization of him as an extremist.[46] And Moussaoui has admitted in court to being a member of al-Qaeda and swearing allegiance to Osama bin Laden.[47] Moussaoui's written pleadings contain similar sentiments. In one motion, Moussaoui wrote, "Everyone knows that I am a dedicated enemy of the United States of America (and of course all its good citizens)." In this, as in his other motions, Moussaoui referred to himself as the "Slave of Allah."[48] At one point during the case, Moussaoui even attempted to plead guilty to four of the six counts charged in the indictment, saying, "I am a member of al-Qaeda. I pledge *bayat* to Osama Bin Ladin."[49] Moussaoui quickly withdrew the plea, however, after the judge explained that he would be accepting responsibility for involvement in the September 11 attacks.[50]

The third factor making terrorism prosecutions so difficult is that these prosecutions are increasingly becoming an international endeavor. Frequently, a terrorist suspect will have traveled to or had ties to numerous countries, and the cooperation of many governments is required for a successful prosecution.[51] Prosecuting terrorists is now a challenge almost without geographical boundaries; according to former CIA Director George Tenet, by February 2002, al-Qaeda operatives had been arrested in more than sixty countries.[52]

The increasingly international aspects of these investigations pose several challenges. First, in the course of an international prosecution, disagreements will often arise between the countries involved. As the cases increase in their international scope, more disagreements are inevitable. A German law professor commented on this phenomenon, noting, "The new terror threat means new types of international legal co-operation are needed. The problem is that we are really only at the beginning of this process."[53] For example, some of the European countries wanted guarantees from the United States that the death penalty would not imposed against terror suspects extradited from Europe. Britain maintained that an extradition without such a guarantee would violate its laws.[54] U.S. Attorney General Ashcroft would not grant a blanket guarantee, arguing that these situations should be dealt with on a "case by case basis.[55]

There are also many cases in which countries do not want their cooperation publicly exposed. Those countries with large Muslim populations, for example, might be concerned about a backlash should their assistance become public. A country might be willing to provide a piece of information, but on the condition that it is used only for intelligence, and not law enforcement, purposes.[56] The country attempting the prosecution would then be left with one of two broad options: it could try to pressure the partner country to allow the public disclosure of the information, or it could attempt to gather the information through other means. If the prosecuting country failed in both pursuits, the terrorism prosecution ultimately might have to be abandoned.

The internationalization of these cases—a phenomenon that began even before September 11—has also opened up a whole new line of probing for the defense. When evidence introduced at trial has been collected by foreign authorities, under rules and procedures that often differ from those of the United States, it is easy for the defense to raise objections of fair process. As former U.S. attorney Mary Jo White has noted, these differences, "although ultimately irrelevant, nevertheless give the defense the ability to appeal to the sympathies of jurors whose sense of fair play and justice is more naturally and instinctively defined on what American law provides and approves."[57] The broader international involvement in these cases has also allowed the defense, at least in Britain, to engage in a wider array of what prosecutors characterize as "fishing expeditions." In at least one case, for example, the defense put forth theories suggesting the existence of an agent provocateur in another country and implying that certain foreign governments involved in the case were actually conspiring to make the defendant appear guilty. The defense then demanded that all government agencies scour their files for evidence to support this theory. Prosecutors believe the function of these defense requests is primarily to plant an element of doubt in the minds of jurors.[58] Some believe that complicated international cases may be unprosecutable in countries such as the United States and Britain, where juries are involved. Even in countries without juries, such as Germany and other continental European countries, the international aspect of these cases remains a significant hurdle for the reasons cited above.

The final factor contributing to the difficulty in prosecuting suspected terrorists is that not all countries have laws that are well designed in this area. While the United States and many European countries have made significant legal changes since September 11, other European countries have not. As will be discussed at greater length below, some European countries have made very few legislative changes since September 11 and therefore have only a very limited capacity to prosecute terrorists. Even in those countries that have made major legislative changes, such as the United States, Britain, Germany and others, the new laws are by no means perfect. Many additional changes could be made in these countries, changes that might improve their capacity to prosecute terrorism cases. Some recommendations for specific changes in counterterrorism law will be discussed later in the study.

As the terrorism threat evolves and as other developments warrant, laws that were once adequate in the United States, Germany, or Britain may become less so. For example, FBI and Justice Department officials grew concerned that there was an increasing danger of a lone individual acting out of sympathy to a formal terrorist group, even if said individual had little or no connection to the group. In their view, this growing phenomenon required a change in law. In the December 2004 intelligence reform bill, Congress increased the FBI's ability to use its intelligence powers to gather information on so-called "lone wolves." Other similar trends in the future and corresponding legislative gaps may also require changes.

Additional legal changes were also made by Congress to account for court rulings that particular terrorism laws were constitutionally problematic, such as the "expert advice and assistance" portion of the material-support-to-terrorism statute. With all of the legal changes that have been made both in the United States and Europe since September 11, it is tempting to consider the changes as largely complete. However, it is important for both the governments and the public to recognize that to adequately address both emerging and ongoing threats, legislative gaps will require additional changes in the future.

No Easy Solution

U.S. and British attempts to handle suspected terrorists through mechanisms outside of the criminal justice system have, in some ways, been even less successful than their efforts at formal prosecution. Both British and U.S. efforts of this type, in addition to being quite controversial, have also encountered serious legal obstacles and may not necessarily represent successful long-term solutions.

British use of indefinite detention and "control orders." As discussed in chapter 2, the British established a system under which they could indefinitely detain in certain circumstances foreign nationals believed to be terrorists. This law required derogation from British obligations under the European Convention for Human Rights (ECHR). In December 2004, the Law Lords found, in response to an appeal from nine such detainees, that Britain's derogation from the ECHR in order to enact this particular law was illegal. The Law Lords concluded that the law itself was both discriminatory and not proportionate to the threat situation, since it only applied to non-British nationals. The Lords ruled that since the derogation was illegal, the Anti-Terrorism, Crime, and Security Act 2000 (ATCSA) was incompatible with Britain's human rights obligations.[59] Britain subsequently replaced Part IV of the act with "control orders" that allow the Home Secretary to place a variety of restrictions on the movement, communication, and associations of suspected terrorists against whom there are "grounds for suspicion."[60] These orders, unlike the Part IV authorities, would apply to both British citizens and foreign nationals and would require independent judicial approval.[61] The individuals subject to the orders are planning to appeal their legality, arguing that the orders violate human rights law.[62] It remains to be seen whether the Law Lords or the European Court of Human Rights in Strasbourg, France, will uphold the legality of the British control orders.

U.S. use of "enemy combatant" status. The legality of the U.S. effort to declare individuals "enemy combatants" and detain them indefinitely has also been the subject of adverse court rulings. The courts have placed limits, for example, on the government's ability to detain U.S. citizens as enemy combatants. Two U.S. citizens held as enemy combatants, Yaser Hamdi and Jose Padilla, had habeas corpus writs filed on their behalf, challenging the legality of their detention. During the protracted litigation in both cases, federal courts at all levels, including the Supreme Court, issued opinions attempting to reign in the executive branch's authority in this arena.

In the Padilla case, the United States Court of Appeals for the Second Circuit ordered the government to either bring criminal charges against him or release him, finding that the president did not have the inherent authority to indefinitely detain a U.S. citizen captured on U.S. soil. This type of action, according to the Second Circuit, would require congressional authorization. The government immediately appealed to the Supreme Court, which declined to rule on the merits of the case, holding instead that Padilla's suit was brought in the wrong jurisdiction and that it should have been filed in South Carolina, not New York. Padilla subsequently refiled his suit in South Carolina. In February 2005, a federal judge there agreed with the Second Circuit, ruling that the government had to either file criminal charges against Padilla or release him within forty-five days. The judge rejected the government's argument that the president has "inherent authority" in this arena, noting that the authority for suspending habeas corpus belongs to Congress and not to the president: "It is true that there may be times during which it is necessary to give the Executive Branch greater power than at other times. Such a granting of power, however, is in the providence of the [legislature] and no one else—not the Court and not the President." The government appealed the judge's ruling.

Hamdi's attorney argued that his client's indefinite detention and inability to seek legal counsel violated his Fifth Amendment right to due process. The government countered that it had the authority during a war to declare individuals as "enemy combatants" and to limit their access to an attorney. Agreeing with Hamdi, the district court instructed the government to release him. The government appealed to the Fourth Circuit, which sided with the government, ruling that courts should give these type of governmental decisions great deference during wartime. Hamdi appealed the ruling to the Supreme Court, which vacated the Fourth Circuit's ruling, finding that Hamdi, as a U.S. citizen, had the right to challenge his detention in court. The Supreme Court sent the case back to the district court for resolution, instructing the lower court to devise a plan consistent with the Supreme Court's ruling. The district court never had the opportunity, however, to determine exactly what were Hamdi's rights. Soon after the Supreme Court's ruling, the United States released Hamdi, sending him back to Saudi Arabia. A Pentagon spokesman stated that the government decided to release Hamdi because "considerations of U.S. national security did not require his continued detention."[63]

The courts have also ruled against some aspects of the government's identification of non-U.S. citizens as enemy combatants. Some background is in order before examining specific rulings. In November 2001, President Bush established a military tribunal to handle the cases of individuals who had been declared by the United States to be enemy combatants. The individuals who were prosecuted were granted certain rights, including the right to counsel, the right to know the charges against them, and the presumption of innocence. Those not charged were not granted these same procedural rights and were not even allowed to challenge their status as "enemy combatants."

In February 2002, relatives of some of those detained as enemy combatants filed suit in U.S. federal court, challenging the legality of the detentions. In June 2004, in *Rasul v. Bush*, the Supreme Court ruled on this matter, holding that federal courts could, in fact, hear detainees' claims that they were being illegally held. The Supreme Court remanded the case to the trial-level courts, to hear the individual detainees' claims. In July 2004, in response to the Supreme Court opinion, the Department of Defense created "Combatant Status Review Tribunals" to review, on an individual basis, each detainee's status as an "enemy combatant." By early 2005, according to the *Washington Post*, the Defense Department had completed its review of 558 of those detained and had taken "final action" in 330 cases, finding that 327 of them were appropriately characterized as "enemy combatants."[64]

In February 2005, Judge Joyce Hens Green of the United States District Court for the District of Columbia ruled that "Combatant Status Review Tribunals" established to hear the detainee claims were unconstitutional, violating detainees' Fifth Amendment rights to due process. Judge Green based her opinion on the detainees' lack of access to the classified information being used against them in these hearings, and the possibility that some of this information might have been obtained through torture. Green concluded that detainees ultimately have the right to have federal courts consider whether they have been illegally detained. The issue of whether the detainees should have access to federal courts will be decided by the federal circuit courts—and possibly by the Supreme Court—because another federal judge hearing a similar case issued a ruling directly contrary to Judge Green's. In ruling against the detainees, this second judge found that their suit had no legal basis.[65]

Backlash

A more aggressive counterterrorism approach—in particular, the emphasis on earlier intervention—by law enforcement and prosecutors, coupled

with the inherent difficulty of proving both to a court and to the public that an individual is guilty of terrorism-related charges, has created
something of a backlash against the governmental actions, particularly
in the United States, but also in Britain. Germans, on the other hand,
have been less critical of their government—perhaps because its efforts
overall have been less far-reaching, particularly in terms of operating
outside the criminal justice system. The U.S. and British governments
have both been accused of exaggerating and politicizing the terrorist
threat, of selectively targeting Muslims for prosecution, and of inflating
counterterrorism successes. A frequent criticism of both governments
is that they have exaggerated the terrorist threat, often for political reasons. In the period leading up to the May 2005 election in Britain, for
example, Prime Minister Tony Blair and his Labor Party were accused of
attempting to create a "climate of fear" in an effort to justify their hard-
line tactics.[66] Both Blair and the Home Secretary had speculated that
Islamic terrorists could—based on their "success" in Spain—attempt an
attack on British targets close to the election date. Blair was also criticized for claiming, in his effort to justify the "control orders," that there
were "several hundred" possible Islamic terrorists in Britain, a figure that
exceeded the earlier estimate of the Home Secretary.[67]

The U.S. government was also heavily criticized for exaggerating the
terrorist threat, particularly before the 2004 election. In August 2004, for
example, the *Washington Post* published an article titled "Don't Politicize
Intelligence," in which the columnist wrote that the presidential election had
created a "vicious cycle of hype, skepticism and mistrust that puts the country's security at risk."[68] Specifically, critics pointed to the timing of particular
threat warnings and the raising of the color-coded homeland security system as evidence that the United States was attempting to manipulate fear of
terrorism for political purposes. Robert Lifton, author of *Superpower Syn-
drome,* stated that warnings have been "associated with difficult or embarrassing moments for the administration." Zbigniew Brzezinski, the former
national security advisor to President Carter, did not go as far in his assessment, but did note, "We are hyping ourselves into a state of panic which is
going to discredit us internationally." He also argued that the use of the "war"
metaphor by both Republicans and Democrats was probably unnecessary.[69]

Both the United States and Britain have been criticized for appearing at
times overly eager to trumpet counterterrorism achievements. The British handling of one case in particular has aroused a great deal of public

condemnation. As discussed in chapter 3, when the British government arrested Kamel Bourgass and other members of an al-Qaeda cell in 2003, accusations began to circulate that traces of the poison ricin had been found during one of the raids. Prime Minister Blair described the arrests as evidence that the danger "is present and real and with us now and its potential is huge."[70] David Blunkett, then Home Secretary, called the cell a threat to the country.[71] Media reports, based on unnamed sources, speculated on the great damage that would have resulted had the attack not been thwarted. In the end, however, it turned out that no actual ricin was found in the apartment, only poison recipes. Only one of the nine defendants was convicted. The verdict and the revelation that no ricin had been found prompted waves of critical articles, with titles such as "Prejudice and Contempt: Terror Trial by Media" and "Exaggerated Threat."[72] Blunkett's public statements during the trial were also criticized by the judge, who noted that the secretary's comments were "clearly in breach of the presumption of innocence."[73]

The United States has likewise been criticized for overhyping specific cases and for inflating its terrorism successes from a statistical perspective. Peter Bergen, a noted al-Qaeda expert, observed that the post–September 11 terrorism cases prosecuted by the United States have "often followed the trajectory of an initial trumpeting by the government only to collapse, or be revealed as something less than earth shattering, when the details emerge months later."[74] In fact, many critics contend that the Justice Department—despite its claims to the contrary—has had few real counterterrorism successes since September 11. For example, in a September 2004 hearing, Senator Patrick Leahy, the ranking member on the Senate Judiciary Committee, stated, "There have really been very few real victories in cases that have brought terrorism charges since Sept. 11 . . . and those seem to have been overshadowed by seemingly half-hearted prosecutions."[75] The critics argue that while the Justice Department can and does point to a number of cases with successful results, with the exception of Richard Reid and Zacarias Moussaoui, there is no evidence that many of the other defendants were involved in terrorism-related activity.[76] The Justice Department disputes this charge, arguing that it is possible that the individuals charged in these terrorism cases—often for material support—might have gone on to commit terrorist attacks had they not been prosecuted. The former head of the Justice Department's criminal division noted, "We would much rather catch a terrorist with his hands on a check than a bomb." Another federal prosecutor stated that though some of the individuals prosecuted might appear to be "bumblers," quite often suicide bombers could be described as bumblers until the day they blow themselves up.[77]

Some critics charge that the Justice Department's preemptive approach to counterterrorism has resulted not in the detention and prosecution of actual terrorists, but in the selective prosecutions of Muslims. In the view of Georgetown University professor David Cole, for example, the government decided that "locking up several thousand foreign nationals is a small price to pay politically" for the privilege of appearing to be aggressively pursuing terrorism. The lawyer for al-Hussayen—the Idaho webmaster who was acquitted of terrorism charges—stated, "If you try to get everybody, then necessarily you're going to get some people who are innocent." The attorney did not believe that the charges against Hussayen would have merited prosecution if the defendant had stood accused of robbery or fraud, and not terrorism.[78]

To bolster their claims, critics have also frequently pointed to a spate of reports since September 11 charging that the Justice Department has statistically inflated its terrorism successes. These reports have been produced by a wide range of entities, including Congress, independent research organizations, and investigative journalists. The first such report was published by the *Philadelphia Inquirer* in December 2001, and stated that the government had been inflating its record of terrorism statistics for years by including crimes that had no relationship to terrorism. "Terrorism" cases, according to the article, included drunk airline passengers, convicts rioting because of prison food, and other nonterrorism-related events.[79] It is important to note that these were not cases of suspected terrorists being prosecuted for nonterrorist offenses; rather, they illustrate an overly broad definition of "terrorism."

A subsequent article in the *Inquirer* made similar charges about the U.S. attorney's office in New Jersey. According to the newspaper, the New Jersey office claimed to have indicted sixty-two individuals with connections to international terrorism in 2002 alone. This was a higher figure than any other jurisdiction in the country. However, the *Inquirer* found that of those sixty-two cases, only one actually belonged under the terrorism label—the murder of *Wall Street Journal* reporter Daniel Pearl. In fact, all but two of the cases were related to Middle Eastern students who had cheated on an English proficiency exam. The U.S. Attorney's office, however, maintained that every one of the cases was properly categorized as involving international terrorism.[80]

In response to the first *Inquirer* article, the federal General Accounting Office (GAO) initiated an investigation into the government's terrorism statistics. The GAO released its report in January 2003, finding that nearly half of the convictions labeled by the Justice Department as terrorism-related were mislabeled. The report concluded that the Department of Justice did not have sufficient management oversight and internal controls in place to ensure the accuracy and reliability of its terrorism-related statistics.[81] A Justice Department spokesman conceded that there were problems with the department's statistics and said that many of the mislabeled cases involved illegal immigrants working at airports. None of those individuals had actually been charged with a terrorism-related offense, though the Justice Department spokesman maintained that "either legal immigrants or illegal immigrants working in sensitive areas of our airport with false documents, that is certainly an attractive avenue for a terrorist."[82]

In December 2003, Syracuse University's Transactional Records Access Clearinghouse (TRAC) released its assessment of the Justice Department's terrorism-related statistics covering the period from September 11 through September 2003. TRAC found that, not surprisingly, the number of terrorism-related prosecutions rose dramatically in that period, when compared to a similar time period before September 11, with terrorism-related convictions rising by more than three-and-a-half times. However, despite the increase in convictions, the number of related individuals receiving sentences of five or more years in prison actually dropped. In fact, according to the study, the median sentence for those convicted of "international terrorism" crimes was only fourteen days.[83]

In 2004, the *Des Moines Register* released the results of its own investigation into the government's terrorism-related statistics. According to the newspaper, federal prosecutors in Iowa claimed thirty-five terrorism cases in the two years after September 11. The *Register* determined, however, that most defendants had "questionable links to violent extremism." In fact, a federal district judge told the daily paper, "If there have been terrorism-related arrests in Iowa, I haven't heard about them." The paper went on to say that among the thirty-five cases were five Mexican citizens who stole cans of baby formula and sold them to an Arab for later resale, and four American-born laborers who failed to mention prior drug convictions and other crimes when assigned to jobs at the Des Moines airport. One federal prosecutor in Iowa said that it was appropriate to include the airport cases in the statistics because the crimes were discovered as part of an initiative to snare potential terrorists.[84]

British counterterrorism statistics have also generated some criticism—though significantly less than in the United States. The primary accusation against the British government has been that its statistics indicate that the government has been engaging in "fishing expeditions" in the terrorism arena. In the view of such critics, the wide disparity between those arrested under the terrorism powers and those actually charged demonstrates that the government is casting too wide a net—often merely targeting members of the Muslim community. As one Muslim leader stated, "Muslims have been targeted and their lives have been tarnished. There is the feeling in the community that they are being victimized." The director of public prosecutions defended the government's efforts, telling a parliamentary committee that the disparity between arrests and charges was inevitable in light of the lower threshold for arrest.[85] A second criticism of British counterterrorism statistics has been that they are substantially less impressive than they appear to be. According to a study by the Institute of Race Relations, Britain's conviction of nearly twenty individuals on charges under the 2000 Terrorism Act is misleading, at least as regards Islamic terrorist groups. Many of those convicted on terrorism-related charges have not been Muslim and were not affiliated with Islamic terrorist groups. For example, six of the twenty were charged with offenses connected to banned Irish terrorist groups, such as the Loyalist Volunteer Force, the Ulster Volunteer Force, and the Ulster Freedom Fighters. Two people convicted under the 2001 act were also non-Muslims. Both pleaded guilty to sending letters with white powder enclosed; one also pleaded guilty to sending racist hate mail.[86]

The greatest criticism in both the United States and Britain has centered on government creation of mechanisms to handle suspected terrorists outside the criminal justice arena. The U.S. decision to house enemy combatants in Guantanamo Bay has been the subject of both domestic and international outrage. The United States has often been accused of abandoning the rule of law, and has been called upon to put these individuals on trial. The creation of military tribunals has done little to quell the controversy. In Britain, the most controversial mechanisms have been the "control orders" and their legislative predecessor—Part IV of the 2001 act, which allowed for the indefinite detention of non-British citizens. The public and media have often been skeptical of the government's claims that the individuals against whom these powers were used are dangerous. In fact, British human rights groups and the media began referring to the indefinite detention provision as "England's Guantanamo."[87] The government was largely ineffective in defending itself against these charges because the intelligence used in the controversial cases was secret.[88] Criticism intensified after several of the special advocates in these cases quit, contending that the process was unfair to the detainees.[89]

Notes

1. Eric Lichtblau, "Trying to Thwart Possible Terrorists Quickly, FBI Agents Are Often Playing Them," *New York Times*, May 30, 2005.

2. David Rummel and Lowell Bergman, "Chasing the Sleeper Cell," *Frontline*, October 16, 2003. Available online (www.pbs.org/wgbh/pages/frontline/shows/sleeper/etc/script. html).

3. Daniel McGrory, "Raids Yield Clues to Europe-Wide Terrorist Network," *Times* (London), January 25, 2003.

4. Craig Whitlock, "Terror Suspects Beating Charges Filed in Europe," *Washington Post*, May 31, 2004.

5. "Prosecutors Refuse to Drop al-Qaeda Terrorism Charges in Berlin," Deutsche Presse-Agentur, August 25, 2004.

6. Mark Trevelyan, "Two Failed Terrorism Trials Raise Worry in Europe," Reuters, April 8, 2005.

7. "A Review of Terrorism Arrests," *Salaam*, May 24, 2004. Available online (www.salaam. co.uk/themeofthemonth/january03_index.php?l=52%82%22=0).

8. Jamie Wilson and Richard Norton-Taylor, "Charges over Plot to Attack Tube," *Guardian* (London), November 18, 2002.

9. Ian Herbert, "Manchester Bewildered As Reports of Chemical Attack Turn Out to Be Untrue," *Independent* (London), April 30, 2004.

10. Criminal complaint, *U.S. v. Yahya Goba*, Western District of New York, September 13, 2002. The six were arrested based on two separate criminal complaints. Five were arrested based on a complaint issued on September 13, 2002, while the sixth was arrested on a separate complaint containing the same charges.

11. *U.S. v. Yahya Goba*; See also *U.S. v. Mukhtar al-Bakri*, October 8, 2002. Both the decisions themselves and the orders to detain the defendants until trial are significant.

12. Susan Candiotti, "Prosecutors: No Bail for Six Accused of Helping al Qaeda," CNN, September 19, 2002. Available online (http://archives.cnn.com/2002/LAW/09/18/buffalo.terror.probe).

13. "Final Member of Alleged Terror Cell in New York Pleads Guilty," Associated Press, May 19, 2003.

14. Ibid.

15. Rummel and Bergman, "Chasing the Sleeper Cell."

16. Kevin Stack, "Chasing Terrorists or Fears? Court Rulings Call the Attorney General's Claims of Homefront Success into Question," *Los Angeles Times*, October 24, 2004.

17. Gary Bald (FBI Assistant Director for Counterterrorism), in written statement before Senate Judiciary Committee, May 6, 2004.

18. For example, Omar Ahmad Ali Abdel Rahman, better known as the "Blind Sheikh," was charged with seditious conspiracy and bombing conspiracy, among other counts, for his role in the New York City "Landmarks" case. Defendants in the first World Trade Center attack were indicted for charges including explosives charges, seditious conspiracy, and bombing conspiracy. Those charged for the bombings of the U.S. embassies in Kenya and Tanzania were indicted on charges including conspiracy to murder Americans, destroying government property, and use of a weapon of mass destruction. Information about all of these cases is available online at www.tkb.org, which is the "Terrorism Knowledge Base" of the National Memorial Institute for the Prevention of Terrorism.

19. Andrew McCarthy, "Winning and Losing," *National Review Online*, June 21, 2004; Mary Jo White (former U.S. Attorney for the Southern District of New York), interview by author, December, 2004. White points out that the great record of success before September 11 was not an indication that the early cases were easy to prosecute. Terrorism cases are always difficult to prosecute, in her view.

20. Trevelyan, "Two Failed Terrorism Trials."

21. Michael Chertoff, "Terrorism and the Law: Approaches to Addressing the Deficiencies Our Legal System Faces When Confronting Terrorism Suspects," speech to the American Bar Association, April 13, 2004. In the speech, Chertoff explained that intelligence information is often hearsay and thus not admissible, or is based on confidential sources that the government does not want to expose.

22. British barrister, interview by author, January 2005.

23. Christoph Safferling, "Terror and Law—Is the German Legal System Able to Deal with Terrorism?" *German Law Journal* 5, no. 5 (May 2004).

24. *United States v. Damrah*, No. 04-4216 (6th Cir., March 15, 2005). In one recent case, the defendant argued that testimony by the government's expert should be inadmissible as

hearsay. The district court denied the defendant's motion, and the appeals court upheld that ruling.

25. Paul Rosenzweig and James Jay Carafano, "Preventive Detention and Actionable Intelligence," Heritage Foundation Legal Memorandum No. 13, September 16, 2004; See also Anti-Terrorism, Crime, and Security Act 2001 Review: Report, Privy Counselor Review Committee, December 18, 2003. The British also have strict hearsay rules, but the Criminal Justice Act of 2003 expanded courts' ability to admit hearsay in situations where it would not be contrary to the interests of justice.

26. "Mystery Still Surrounds Killer," BBC News, April 13, 2005. Available online (http://newswww.bbc.net.uk/1/hi/uk/4440953.stm).

27. Eric Lichtblau, "Charity Leader Accepts a Deal in Terror Case," *New York Times*, February 10, 2003.

28. "Muslim Charity Director Tried on Terror Funding Case," CNN, February 10, 2003. Available online (www.cnn.com/2003/US/Midwest/02/10/attacks.charities.ap).

29. Lichtblau, "Charity Leader Accepts a Deal."

30. Michael Weissenstein, "Federal Judge Undercuts Government Case Set to Open Thursday against Yemeni Sheikh," Associated Press, January 25, 2005.

31. *CIA v. Sims*, 471 US 159, 176 (1985). As far as why the decision is better left to the government than to the court, one court found that "whether an intelligence source will be harmed if his identity is revealed will often require complex political, historical, and psychological judgments," judgments that courts are ill equipped to make.

32. *U.S. v. Moussaoui*, quoting *United States v. Rezaq*, 134 F.3d 1121, 1143 (D.C. Cir., 1998). In the United States, CIPA allows the government to propose substitutions for classified information. The district court must accept the substitution as long as it provides the defendant "with substantially the same ability to make his defense as would disclosure of the specific classified information." Under PII, the judge will weigh the government's need to protect sensitive information with the defendant's right to have access to all relevant material. Unlike CIPA, PII does not have a system of structured disclosures. The information is either excluded or included, and governmental changes or substitutions are not permitted. For more information, read about the Crown Prosecution Service (details available online at www.cps.gov/uk/legal/section20/chapter_i.html).

33. The document is available on the Department of Justice website (www.usdoj.gov/ag/trainingmanual.htm).

34. "Guide for Terrorists in Embassy Case," Associated Press, April 5, 2001; Alan Feuer and Benjamin Wiser, "Translation: 'The How-To Book of Terrorism'," *New York Times*, April 5, 2001. Illustrating how difficult the balancing act that the U.S. government faces in this regard, the Department of Justice has only uploaded a portion of the manual on its website because "it does not want to aid in educating terrorists or encourage further acts of terrorism" (the edited manual is available at www.usdoj.gov/ag/trainingmanual.htm).

35. 9-11 Commission, *Final Report*, p. 472.

36. Dan Benjamin and Steve Simon, *The Age of Sacred Terror* (New York: Random House, 2002), pp. xii, xiii.

37. "Berlin Court Acquits Tunisian Garnaoui of Planning Bomb Attacks," Bloomberg News Service, April 6, 2005.

38. "Law Lords Review Terror Detention," BBC News, October 4, 2004. Available online (http://news.bbc.co.uk/2/hi/uk_news/3712318.stm).

39. Anti-Terrorism, Crime, and Security Act 2001 Review.

40. For quite some time, few details were known about the case. In April 2004, Senator Orrin Hatch, the chairman of the Senate Judiciary Committee, sent a letter to the attorney general asking for more information about U.S. citizens being held as enemy combatants. In June 2004, prompted in part by this request, Deputy Attorney General James Comey held a press conference to outline the government's case against Jose Padilla.

41. "Transcript of News Conference on Jose Padilla," CNN, June 1, 2004. Available online (www.cnn.com/2004/LAW/06/01/comey.padilla.transcript).

42. "Transcript of News Conference on Jose Padilla."

43. *U.S. v. Zacarias Moussaoui*, Opinion of the United States Court of Appeals for the Fourth Circuit, September 13, 2004.

44. *U.S. v. Zacarias Moussaoui*, Opinion of the Court.

45. Jerry Markon, "Moussaoui Asks Supreme Court to Ban al Qaeda Witnesses," *Washington Post*, January 11, 2005.

46. Philip Shenon, "Terror Suspect Says He Wants U.S. Destroyed," *New York Times*, April 23, 2002.

47. Phil Hirschkorn, "Judge Rejects Federal Proposal in Moussaoui Case," CNN, April 24, 2003 (available online at www.cnn.com/2003/LAW/04/24/Moussaoui); Phil Hirschkorn, "Stand-by Lawyer for Moussaoui Named," CNN, June 18, 2002 (available online at http://archives.cnn.com/2002/LAW/06/17/moussaoui.trial). In fact, Moussaoui also attacked the judge on several occasions, writing, "She must be dismiss (sic) for her own mental interest. . . . P.S. the curse of Allah is and be on you." Hirschkorn, "Stand-by Lawyer."

48. Ibid.

49. Dahlia Lithwick, "Terrorism on Trial," *Slate*, July 18, 2002. Available online (http://slate.msn.com/id/2066986/entry/2068340).

50. "Moussaoui Drops Guilty Plea," BBC News, July 25, 2002. Moussaoui accepted the charge that he provided a guesthouse and training, and he pleaded guilty to the contents of the indictment. He emphasized, however, that these admissions did not put him "on the plane."

51. For example, in the Badat case, British authorities traveled to fifteen different countries as part of the investigation. In another British counterterrorism case, the investigation has spanned twenty-six different countries. Author interview with Peter Clarke, January 2005.

52. John Lumpkin, "CIA: About 1,000 al-Qaida Arrested," Associated Press, February, 2002.

53. Edward Alden, Nikki Tait, et al., "Legal Cases in Germany and the US Show How Authorities with Interests That Often Diverge Are Inching towards Greater Co-Operation in Prosecuting Suspects," *Financial Times*, October 7, 2004.

54. Nicholas Watt, Richard Norton-Taylor, et al., "Europe Urged to End Hostility to US Death Penalty," *Guardian* (London), December 13, 2001.

55. "Ashcroft Questioned on Death Penalty," CNN, December 12, 2001. Available online (http://archives/cnn.com/2001/world/europe/12/12/gen.ashcroft.blunkett).

56. Jane Meyer, "Outsourcing Torture," *New Yorker*, February 14, 2005.

57. Mary Jo White, "Prosecuting Terrorism in New York," *Middle East Quarterly* 8, no. 2 (Spring 2001). Available online (www.meforum.org/article/25).

58. Peter Clarke, interview by author, January 2005.

59. "Opinion of the Lords of Appeal for Judgment in the Cause of A (FC) and others (FC) (Appellants) v. Secretary of State for the Home Department," December 16, 2004.

60. Alan Cowell, "Bitter Political Duel in Britain over New Anti-Terror Legislation," *New York Times*, March 9, 2005.

61. According to a "Frequently Asked Questions" section formerly posted on the Home Office website (www.homeoffice.gov.uk).

62. Robert Verkaik, "Terror Suspects' Lawyers Challenge Control Orders," *New Zealand Herald*, March 15, 2005. Available online (www.nzherald.co.nz/index.cfm?c_id=2&ObjectID=10115369).

63. Jerry Markon, "Hamdi Returned to Saudi Arabia," *Washington Post*, October 12, 2004.

64. Carol D. Leonnig, "Judge Rules Tribunals Illegal," *Washington Post*, February 1, 2005.

65. Ibid.

66. Bob Glanville, "Britain—Blair Accused of Hyping Terror Threat," *Morning Star*, April 5, 2005.

67. Patrick O'Flynn, "MI5 Protest That Blair 'Sexed Up' Terrorist Claims," *Express*, March 2, 2005.

68. David Ignatius, "Don't Politicize Intelligence," *Washington Post*, August 17, 2004.

69. "A False Sense of Insecurity," *Pittsburgh Post-Gazette*, September 12, 2004.

70. "Exaggerated Threats," *Guardian* (London), April 14, 2005.

71. Nick Cohen, "How to Stitch Up a Terror Suspect," *Observer* (London), January 12, 2003.

72. "Exaggerated Threats"; see also Arun Kundnani, "Prejudice and Contempt: Terror Trial by Media," Institute of Race Relations (IRR) news network, January 1, 2003 (available online at www.irr.org.uk/2003/january/ak000019.html).

73. Pat Clarke, "Judge Censures Blunkett over Ricin Trial," Press Association, April 13, 2005.

74. Peter Bergen, "Islamic Extremism in Europe," in testimony before the House Committee on International Relations, April 27, 2005; D. Mark Jackson, "Has Attorney General John Ashcroft, in Alleged Terrorism Cases, Violated Government Ethics Rules Governing Prosecutors' Comments about the Accused?" FindLaw, January 30, 2003 (available online at http://writ.corporate.findlaw.com/commentary/20030130_jackson.html). Former Attorney General Ashcroft has been the object of most of this criticism. In all of these cases, Ashcroft has held press conferences and made public statements. Critics have charged that Ashcroft has made statements that have prejudiced the defendants' ability to receive a fair trial. Jackson stated that Ashcroft's comments in these cases had "no serious prosecutorial or law enforcement purpose. Their apparent purpose was to serve as part of a public relations campaign with the intent of increasing political support for the actions of the administration, and silencing potential critics."

75. Stack, "Chasing Terrorists or Fears?"

76. See, for example, a February 2005 study by the NYU Center on Law and Security.

77. Stack, "Chasing Terrorists or Fears?"

78. Ibid.

79. Mark Fazlollah and Peter Nicholas, "US Overstates Arrests in Terrorism," *Philadelphia Inquirer*, December 16, 2001.

80. Mark Fazlollah, "Terrorism Statistics Inflated in NJ," *Philadelphia Inquirer*, March 2, 2003.

81. "Justice Department: Better Management Oversight and Internal Controls Needed to Ensure Accuracy of Terrorism-Related Statistics," GAO, Summary of Study, January 17, 2003.

82. Mark Fazlollah, "Antiterror Success Found Overstated," *Philadelphia Inquirer*, February 21, 2003.

83. "Criminal Terrorism Enforcement since the 9/11/01 Attacks," TRAC Special Report, December 8, 2003. Available online (http://trac.syr.edu/tracreports/terrorism/report031208.html).

84. Bert Dalmer, "Many of Bush Administration's Claimed 'Terrorism' Arrests Are Misleading," *Des Moines Register*, July 18, 2004.

85. Philip Johnston, "Most Suspects Will Be Free in a Week," *Daily Telegraph* (London), August 5, 2004.

86. Harmit Athwal, "Analysis: Who Are the Terrorists?" IRR, August 12, 2004. Available online (http://www.irr.org.uk/2004/august/ak000007.html).

87. Iain S. Bruce, "Join the Club: The Top Ten Other Regimes That Imprison without Trial," *Sunday Herald* (Glasgow), March 6, 2005.

88. Audrey Gillan, "No Names, No Charges, No Explanations: The Plight of Britain's Interned 'Terrorists,'" *Guardian* (London), September 9, 2002.

89. "QC Quits over 'Flawed' Terror Laws," *Birmingham Post*, December 20, 2004; Aida Edemariam, "Portrait: It's Britain's Guantanamo," *Guardian* (London), January 20, 2005.

Conclusion

FROM THE PERSPECTIVE OF U.S. POLICYMAKERS, THE problems identified in this book have no easy solutions. It is a difficult enough challenge for the United States to resolve the thorny issues associated with its own efforts to prosecute suspected terrorists, let alone work with European countries to address their problems. However, given that U.S. national security depends in part on the effectiveness of European counterterrorism efforts, the United States must attempt to succeed on both fronts. On the latter front, there are several ways in which American policymakers should work with the Europeans on these issues.

1. Focus on commonalities.

The United States must work to overcome the perception that its counterterrorism efforts have been at odds with Europe's since September 11. Otherwise, working closely together to resolve these overarching difficulties will be next to impossible. The United States should make an effort to demonstrate that the two sides are not as far apart in their approaches to fighting terrorism as has been publicly portrayed. Focusing on similarities in counterterrorism approaches and in mutual difficulties would hopefully go a long way toward demonstrating to skeptical U.S. and European audiences that such portrayals have often been two-dimensional. For example, it would help reassure the U.S. public that Germany has taken major steps in its counterterrorism efforts since September 11. It might also help counter the German—and broader European—public perception that the United States has abandoned the rule of law and is only using military means to fight terror. A focus on common ground should make it far easier for both sides of the Atlantic to collaboratively tackle their similar problems.

2. Initiate strategic collaboration on counterterrorism.

Despite the fact that the United States and Europe have encountered many of the same problems with regard to terrorism, there has been little effort to collaborate on solutions. It is essential that Washington work closely with the EU and its member states on these issues. Senior policymakers on both sides of the Atlantic should focus on determining whether overarching solutions can be developed. This is not to imply that the United States and European countries have failed to cooperate on individual investigations or prosecutions. In fact, cooperation at the tactical level has often been excellent. Collaboration at the strategic level, however, is another story.

In addition to high-level policymaking attention, the parties should convene a commission to focus on strategic issues, to include representatives of the United States, the European Union, and EU member states. This commission should be mandated to review U.S. and European states' law enforcement and prosecution efforts in the counterterrorism arena since September 11. It should review not only individual cases and operations, but also the effectiveness of the countries' overarching law enforcement and prosecutorial strategy. In areas where the United States and Europe have faced similar difficulties, the commission should propose common solutions. Of course, a "one size fits all" solution will not always make sense. Still, the more the United States and Europe can adopt similar laws, strategies, and approaches, the more effectively they will be able to work with each other.

Several examples help illustrate how Washington could focus its efforts in this regard. In terms of counterterrorism strategy, the United States, Britain, and Germany have all discovered links between terrorism and criminal activity. Due to the difficulties inherent in prosecuting terrorism-related cases, all three have adopted the approach—independently, by all accounts—of prosecuting terrorists for nonterrorism-related crimes.[1] This strategy has proven effective in cases where terrorist suspects might otherwise have walked free. The United States should work in consultation with Germany and Britain to ensure that other European countries are embracing this approach, investigating the potential overlap between terrorism and crime and taking advantage of such linkages in their prosecutorial efforts. These countries should also be encouraged to reform other aspects of their counterterrorism efforts. As discussed at length in this study, the United States, Britain, and Germany have increasingly centralized their counterterrorism structures, prioritized counterterrorism among their law enforcement agencies and prosecutors, and improved cooperation and coordination between their domestic intelligence and law enforcement agencies. Other European countries could greatly strengthen their counterterrorism capabilities by adopting similar changes.

Washington should also encourage European countries to increase their focus on prosecuting "material support" cases. As discussed earlier, material support legislation has been the cornerstone of U.S. efforts to prosecute suspected terrorists. The United States must push Europe to take aggressive action against not only terrorist operatives and leaders, but also those providing financial, logistical, or other support to terrorist groups. Some European countries may already have adequate laws on the books, requiring only external pressure to make active use of these laws. In other countries, legislative changes may be needed to criminalize material support activity.

Even if it ultimately proved too difficult for the United States or European countries to adopt any aspect of each other's counterterrorism approaches, collaboration would have other side benefits. For example, the United States might gain insight into prosecuting suspected terrorists from countries such as Spain, France, and Britain—states that have been dealing with this issue for decades. In combating terrorist groups, these European countries have learned valuable lessons, some of which are undoubtedly applicable against today's threat. European countries could also learn a great deal from the United States, since Europe's counterterrorism efforts remain extremely uneven. To be sure, some European countries are greatly concerned about terrorism and have robust intelligence and law enforcement capabilities in addition to fairly well-developed legal regimes. Other countries are less focused, however. The United States must therefore take advantage of any opportunity to work with European countries, whether they possess strong or weak counterterrorism capabilities. The latter may prove less valuable in terms of "lessons learned" from the U.S. perspective, but improving these nations' counterterrorism capabilities and legal regimes would have enormous potential benefits for both European and U.S. security. Washington must do what it can, in this context, to ensure that all European countries—not just the most obvious targets—are aware of the magnitude of the terrorist threat. This may require that the United States provide European governments with sensitive intelligence and intelligence assessments, but in many cases this is a risk worth taking. Intelligence on terrorist groups' interest in acquiring and using weapons of mass destruction would be particularly powerful in driving home the point that terrorism is a global threat.

Another benefit of collaboration would be increased understanding of U.S. and European counterterrorism systems and approaches. Understanding improves cooperation and helps allies better relate to each other when disagreements arise.

3. Improve tactical cooperation.

Although tactical counterterrorism cooperation between the United States and Europe has been good since September 11, it could certainly be improved further. It is becoming increasingly difficult to successfully prosecute terrorist suspects without cooperation from foreign governments. Therefore, it is essential that all parties work to remove any existing obstacles to cooperation in the law enforcement or prosecution arenas. For example, in order to provide intelligence to European authorities for use in terrorism prosecutions, the United States must have confidence that the European system will permit adequate protection of classified information during the course of these trials. While the U.S. Classified Information Procedures Act (CIPA) may not fit into European civil law structures, there are certainly changes that European countries can make to provide greater protection for classified information in terrorism prosecutions.

In addition, these countries could help eliminate U.S. hesitance about trying suspects in Europe by lengthening their sentences for terrorism convictions. The United States, in turn, should consider removing the death penalty as an option for terrorism prosecutions in which international cooperation is needed. Capital punishment is a particularly serious issue for many European countries, and they are often reluctant to cooperate in situations where they believe their assistance would lead to a death sentence.

4. Encourage the European Union to play a greater role.

Although many critics are dismissive of the EU's role in the national security arena, it is nonetheless important that the United States work closely not only with the individual member states, but with the European Union as an entity. Where possible, the United States should push the EU to assume a greater role in European counterterrorism operations, for several reasons. First, the European member states' counterterrorism efforts are extremely uneven. While some countries, such as France, Spain, and Britain, take the threat very seriously and have fairly strong intelligence and law enforcement capabilities, this is not the case across the board. The EU might be in the best position to push laggard countries to improve their domestic counterterrorism capabilities. In fact, there are many instances where countries welcome pressure from the EU, as it allows them to take actions that their populations might otherwise oppose. Spain has used this technique on a number of occasions. It has been pushing for improved information sharing mechanisms to be created on an EU level. There has been speculation that Spain is interested in this issue because its ultimate goal is to improve domestic information sharing between intelligence and law enforcement agencies.[2]

Second, cooperation and coordination on counterterrorism within Europe remains problematic. The EU is in a better position to improve this situation than is the United States or any individual member state. The United States will likely find Germany a willing partner in efforts to involve the EU in this process. After September 11, Germany pushed for grid-searching at the European level. The Germans were also a leading force in advocating for the European Arrest Warrant (EAW).[3] German Interior Minister Otto Schily has been pressing for a European-wide network of agencies that would facilitate information sharing between national intelligence and police services.[4]

The British, on the other hand, are likely to be quite resistant to any effort to increase the EU's role or power in the national security arena. Britain has opposed, for example, proposals to establish a European public prosecutor and to increase the power of Europol and Eurojust. David Blunkett, the former home secretary, stated that under no circumstances could he envision the creation of a European public prosecutor.[5] There has also been significant domestic opposition in Britain to the EAW. For example, a parliamentary committee described the measure as "deeply disturbing," citing hypothetical examples of cases in which its use might be problematic.[6]

In addition to encouraging institutional pressure, Washington should call on EU member states with stronger counterterrorism capabilities to spur states with weaker capabilities toward improvement. In this regard, the United States should take advantage of the "bureacractic peer pressure" that counterterrorism expert Jonathan Stevenson claims is prevalent in Europe.[7] According to him, this internal pressure to adopt a more aggressive approach reflects an understanding that al-Qaeda-inspired terrorist attacks have the potential to be far more catastrophic than the "old-style" terrorist activity that has long persisted in Europe.

U.S. policymakers should also take steps independently of Europe:

1. Consider legislative solutions for prosecutions of suspected terrorists to the greatest extent possible.

The United States should consider whether there are legislative solutions, including fundamental reform of the criminal justice system, that would allow it to effectively prosecute all suspected terrorists. Until now—perhaps in anticipation of the challenges inherent in such proposals—the U.S. government has not proposed or even considered any major legislative overhauls of the criminal justice system in order to better accommodate terrorism prosecutions; the system itself appears to be regarded as sancrosanct.[8] But there are a broad range of legislative proposals—both broad and far-reaching and more narrowly tailored—that the administration could consider. In terms of more fundamental reform, a number of experts on both the right and the left have called on Congress to create a specialized court with sole jurisdiction over terrorism prosecutions. The argument for such a court is that criminal courts are not designed for, or capable of handling, complex terrorism prosecutions. The proponents of a terrorism court maintain that it would allow the government to use intelligence information more easily in trials while at the same time better protecting sources and methods. The greatest challenge inherent in this proposal would be creating a system that comports with the Constitution (assuming that the country is unwilling to amend the Constitution), particularly given the requirements of the Sixth Amendment, which entitles every defendant to a fair trial. Under that amendment, defendants have the right to an attorney, to a speedy trial, to confront the prosecution's witnesses, and to see the evidence being used against them.[9] Senate Judiciary Chairman Arlen Specter, however, has proposed to make use of an existing judicial entity—the FISA Court—to hear the cases of individuals who have been detained without trial.[10]

Other experts believe, for example, that Congress should enact a narrowly tailored and highly managed preventive detention regime, similar to the systems currently in place in France, Spain, and other European countries.[11] Democratic Senator Charles Schumer is among those to suggest that the United States might need to consider alternative approaches to dealing with terrorism suspects. In the case of one individual who was deported, Schumer said that a better approach might have been to consider options such as a classified criminal trial.[12] As with the proposals above, either of these options would have to be carefully designed so as not to run afoul of the Constitution. A classified criminal trial could potentially violate a defendant's Sixth Amendment rights to see the evidence and confront the witnesses against him, and preventive detention could violate the Fourth Amendment right against unreasonable search and seizure.[13]

While making significant changes to our system within the bounds of the Constitution presents a difficult challenge, a variety of serious proposals have been floated that to this point have received little attention. Given that the United States is now several years into the "war on terror," with no end in sight, it is time for the government to acknowledge this by thinking longer-term as it combats terrorism. In fact, to this point, there has been little U.S. public debate on this issue. While there has certainly been heated debate over the Patriot Act and the detention center at Guantanamo Bay, little has been said about making fundamental changes to the criminal justice system so that it can be used more effectively to prosecute suspected terrorists. Although enacting this type of fundamental reform may not be the right solution, considering legislative solutions—and having a public debate on this issue—would nonetheless be important. First and foremost, it would help demonstrate that the United States is highly concerned about adhering to the rule of law, and might help alleviate some of the two-dimensional portrayals of the United States running rampant in some parts of the world. Second, the United States might discover, in the course of such a review, that there are a variety of smaller, less overarching changes that can be made. Third, learning more about how other countries handle similar issues would be beneficial for both U.S. policymakers and the public.

The call for a public debate in the United States on these issues is now coming from a variety of sources—and the U.S. administration should heed it. For example, in an April 2004 speech, Michael Chertoff, the current head of the Department of Homeland Security, argued that whether or not the United States ultimately decides to make sweeping changes, the time for the public debate, at least, has come. Chertoff expressed support for the idea of looking to other Western democracies, such as France and Britain, for ideas on improving the U.S. system.[14]

Others on all sides of the political spectrum have called for the administration—and perhaps even more important, for Congress—to devise a long-term legislative strategy on these issues. In an April 20, 2005, editorial, the *Washington Post* pointed to court rulings regarding the military tribunals and the Moussaoui case as evidence that the current approach is not working. The *Post* opined that the administration has been too reluc-

tant to solve these issues through legislation and called on Congress to
"clarify the rules" regarding federal terrorism prosecutions and military
tribunals.[15] The president of the National Institute of Military Justice made
a similar point, but leveled his criticism for the lack of legislative action
directly at Congress: "Congress' failure to play a role in any of these issues
has been extremely unfortunate and an erosion of their responsibilities."[16]

2. Remove the politics from counterterrorism prosecutions.

As was discussed at length earlier in the study, U.S. officials have held
press conferences and issued numerous public statements in many of the
post–September 11 prosecutions. They have also trumpeted counterterrorism statistics as a sign that the government is effectively rooting out terrorists and bringing them to justice. When these prosecutions have either
failed or come up short, or the statistics have been revealed as exaggerated, the government's credibility has been damaged. To succeed in their
counterterrorism efforts, prosecutors and law enforcement officials must
be viewed as nonpolitical actors. If judges—and worse, juries—regard the
government's counterterrorism efforts as politicized, the government is
likely to encounter great difficulties. To address these issues, the U.S. government should:

- Make as few public comments about counterterrorism cases as possible
  until after conviction. Let indictments speak for themselves.

- Be far more cautious in use of counterterrorism statistics. The government should take great care to ensure that these statistics are accurate
  and not exaggerated in any way. And while it is important to release
  such data, trumpeting it publicly often gives it political overtones.

In this second regard, the United States might take a lesson from Britain.
The British have not publicly promoted their counterterrorism cases as
aggressively as has the United States.[17] Therefore, when difficulties arise,
they do not have the same type of impact on the government's credibility; the government has not staked its credibility to the same extent on
the success of these cases. British reticence to promote its cases is due, in
large part, to strict contempt-of-court laws. The 1981 Contempt of Court
Act prohibits the publication of any information, from the time of arrest,
that might affect a case. This obligation is taken seriously, and when Brit-

ish officials have made what are deemed to be inappropriate comments, they have been heavily criticized. In one pre–September 11 case, a British official was forced to resign after making inappropriate comments about a defendant.[18] Beyond the restrictions in individual cases, the British are generally reluctant to provide information about the terrorist threat more generally, believing that this type of information would be useful to terrorists and ought not be released. While it is certainly understandable that U.S. government officials would want to defend their efforts against attacks, perhaps the British can offer a lesson as to why, from a long-term perspective, this is not always the best course of action.

3. Ensure that prosecutors are sufficiently independent from law enforcement.

One of the most important U.S. developments after September 11 has been that prosecutors and law enforcement officers now work far more closely on counterterrorism investigations. Before September 11, the "wall" between intelligence and criminal investigations prevented these relationships from developing. But a downside of the closer relationship is that prosecutors may lose some of their independent perspective, and be more likely to be advocates for particular cases instead of acting as objective reviewers. The United States must find a way to maintain these close ties while ensuring that prosecutors are able to make objective judgments about the strengths of the investigators' cases. Here, too, the United States could look to Britain for guidance. The British Crown Prosecution Service (CPS)—the rough equivalent of the U.S. Justice Department—is far more independent from British law enforcement than is the Justice Department from the FBI. CPS lawyers are less intimately involved in counterterrorism investigations than are U.S. prosecutors. CPS agents, who serve as the filter mechanism for the work of law enforcement, regard their independence from law enforcement as vital; from CPS's perspective, the less involved agents are in the actual investigations, the more dispassionate and objective they will be in deciding the merits of cases. If CPS were to lose this objectivity, it would be concerned that judges, in particular, would no longer have the same faith in its prosecutorial judgments.[19] While there are many positives to the United States' post–September 11 approach—in which prosecutors are integral members of investigative teams—finding ways to ensure that prosecutors maintain their independence would be an important step in improving the Justice Department's credibility.

Notes

1. Andreas Tzortzis, "The Trouble with Nailing Terror Suspects," Deutsche Welle, April 8, 2005. Available online (www.dw-world.de/dw/article/0,1564,1545583,00.html).

2. Author interview with senior EU official, January 2005.

3. Oliver Lepsius, "Liberty, Security and Terrorism: The Legal Position in Germany, Part 1 and 2," *German Law Journal* 5, no. 5 (May 2004).

4. "Report to the Security Council Committee Established Pursuant to Resolution 1373 (2001) concerning Counterterrorism."

5. Author interview with senior EU official, January 2005.

6. Andrew Sparrow, "EU Warrants 'Undermine British Law,'" *Telegraph* (London), March 17, 2005.

7. Jonathan Stevenson, *Counter-Terrorism: Containment and Beyond* (Adelphi Paper 367) (London: International Institute for Strategic Studies, 2004).

8. Mary Jo White (U.S. Attorney), interview by author, December 2004; Ruth Wedgwood, "Prosecuting Al Qaeda: September 11 and Its Aftermath," Crimes of War Project, December 7, 2001 (available online at www.crimesofwar.org/expert/al-wedgwood.html). Leading figures outside the government also oppose this type of reform. For example, one of the foremost terrorism prosecutors in the country, former U.S. Attorney Mary Jo White, does not believe that we should make fundamental changes to our criminal justice system. In her view, that would undermine the system. Rather, we should design better military tribunals. White noted that while many people believe that a military court is the equivalent of a "kangaroo court," the military tribunal conviction rate of approximately 80 percent is lower than the Southern District of New York's pre–September 11 conviction rate of 100 percent in terrorism trials. Yale University professor Ruth Wedgewood agrees that the United States should handle al-Qaeda prosecutions through military tribunals, which she notes are a "time honored legal recourse for times of war."

9. Andrew C. McCarthy, "Abu Ghraib & Enemy Combatants: An Opportunity to Draw Good out of Evil," *National Review Online*, May 11, 2004; Thomas Powers, "Due Process for Terrorists," *Weekly Standard*, January 12, 2004. McCarthy, a former federal prosecutor, proposed that a specialized national security court—similar to the one now in place to hear FISA applications—be established, which would have jurisdiction over individuals detained as unlawful combatants. These courts would be Article III courts, not military tribunals, though the proceedings would more closely resemble military tribunals. McCarthy also argues that tightening the government's obligations under *Brady v. Maryland* (373 US 83 [1963]) to disclose to the defense exculpatory information would be helpful. According to McCarthy, the Brady obligations have been interpreted in an increasingly broad fashion over the years, and now include "much that is neither exculpatory, admissible nor particularly germane but that might be thought helpful to

the defense presentation." This idea for a separate court was also put forth by Thomas Powers, a constitutional law professor at the University of Minnesota, who noted that this type of institutional reform was supported by a variety of leading voices on both the left and the right. In Powers's view, defendants under a separate court would have specially appointed attorneys with security clearances, would know the charges against them, and would have the right of appeal. The court would have its own evidentiary rules that allow for better protection of sensitive information and sources. Powers also argues that there is precedent in the United States for this type of system, saying that its creation would be roughly analogous to the 1978 establishment of the FISA courts. The judges would have lifetime appointments, as do all other federal judges. Powers notes that most of the support for this idea comes from the left, including Burt Neuborne, former director of the ACLU. Supporters on the right, according to Powers, include former high-level Justice Department officials such as Michael Chertoff, who also appear to support fundamental change.

10. Charlie Savage, "Push on to Clarify Rights for Detainees," *Boston Globe*, May 31, 2005.

11. Paul Rosenzweig and James Jay Carafano, "Preventive Detention and Actionable Intelligence," Heritage Foundation Legal Memorandum no. 13, September 16, 2004; Benjamin Wittes, "Enemy Americans," *Atlantic Monthly*, July/August 2004; Stuart Taylor, "The Fragility of Our Freedoms in a Time of Terror," *National Journal*, May 5, 2004. Under Rosenzweig and Carafano's approach, the statute would be limited to terrorism cases, and would have rigorous certification procedures, subject to the approval of both the attorney general and the courts.

12. John Soloman, "Terror Suspect Deport Raises Fuss," Associated Press, June 30, 2004. Available online (www.cbsnews.com/stories/2004/06/03/terror/main620825.shtml).

13. Paul Rosenzweig, interview by author; Viet Dinh, interview by author. Rosenzweig believes that due process and the Fourth Amendment "reasonableness" standards are flexible enough to permit a narrowly tailored preventive detention scheme without constitutional changes. For example, courts have already held that it is constitutional for defendants to be denied bail and detained until trial, which is similar from a constitutional perspective to preventive detention. Viet Dinh agrees that it may be possible to craft a constitutional preventive detention system, but only one that is strictly limited in duration. The speedy trial requirements, Dinh notes, would pose an additional constraint in this regard. Dinh believes that there is an even more difficult issue to address should the United States undertake fundamental reform of its criminal justice system—namely, the government must find a way to accommodate the disclosure requirements of the Sixth Amendment and other laws in a manner that gives defendants constitutionally adequate access to the witnesses and evidence against them, but that does not compromise U.S. national security. Such a balancing act will be difficult, in Dinh's view, though not necessarily impossible. According to Dinh, any such alternative system would derive from the president's authority as commander-in-chief, and not from relaxation of the criminal justice requirements.

14. Michael Chertoff, "Terrorism and the Law: Approaches to Addressing the Deficiencies Our Legal System Faces When Confronting Terrorism Suspects," speech to the American Bar Association, April 13, 2004.

15. "A September 11 Plea?" *Washington Post*, April 20, 2005.

16. Savage, "Push on to Clarify Rights."

17. Gareth Crossman, interview by author, January 2005. The senior official from the British civil rights group Liberty believes that the British population also has more of an inherent trust in the integrity of its government officials; the public generally believes that the government will act in the best interests of the population.

18. Arun Kundnani, "Prejudice and Contempt: Terror Trial by Media," IRR, January 1, 2003 (available online at www.irr.org.uk/2003/january/ak00019.html); Peter Clarke, interview by author, January 2005. For example, after Sajid Badat was arrested, Home Secretary David Blunkett referred to him as a "very real threat to the life and liberty of our country." The attorney general investigated these remarks, but ultimately cleared Blunkett. The British, not surprisingly, do not view the contempt of court law in such a positive light, maintaining that it makes it difficult for them to defend their counterterrorism efforts against criticism by the defendant's supporters, civil liberties groups, and the general public.

19. British barrister, interview by author, January, 2005.